My Wolf Fighter

Wolf Town Guardians
Book 4

Rose Wynters

Copyright Notice

This is a work of fiction. All characters, organizations, and events listed in this book are products of the author's imagination or used fictitiously. The author acknowledges the trademark status and trademark ownership of all trademarks, service marks, and/or word marks (if any) mentioned in this book.

My Wolf Fighter (Wolf Town Guardians, Book 4)

All Rights Reserved

© 2014 Rose Wynters

No parts of this book may be used, scanned, duplicated, copied, or reproduced without written permission from the author, with the exception of small quotations used in reviews or articles.

This book has been provided for your personal enjoyment only. Sharing or posting publicly is strictly prohibited.

Get updates on new releases, giveaways, and sales at:

http://www.rosewynters.com

Chapter 1

"I'm sorry, but our tests are clear. You have pancreatic cancer."

Tears streamed down Amanda's face as she sat in her car, replaying the doctor's words over and over again. He'd said quite a bit in that brief time, but her mind wasn't capable of moving past the diagnosis. She blinked hard, her throat and nose clogged with tears. She was only twenty-nine, but she had cancer. A very deadly form of cancer, if the doctor's tests could be believed.

Her hand hovered over the small, worn purse that contained her cell phone, but who could she call? Her parents were dead, having passed away in their first and only trip to New York during the twin towers tragedy. Her last surviving relative was an older sister, but they'd never been close, especially as adults. Tina was too self-absorbed to care about anyone but herself. They hadn't spoken since the funeral and barely even then.

Calling her boyfriend, Jimmy, was out of the question. Although they lived together, their relationship was strained. Amanda felt as if she were barely holding onto it by a strand. A very worn, frayed strand that was growing thinner by the day. As a truck driver, Jimmy was usually only home on the weekends, but sometimes not even then. In the back of her mind, she suspected he was cheating on her again. Jimmy always got meaner when he cheated. Lately, he'd been meaner than a rattlesnake. Nothing she did pleased him.

Amanda sighed, her chin dropping down to her chest in weariness. Time and time again she considered leaving him, but where would she go? And how would she pay for it? Even working full-time as a bartender, she barely cleared minimum wage. It certainly wasn't enough to pay the full rent and utilities on a new place, and God only knew how much her treatments would cost. Especially considering she was uninsured. One thing was certain. Moving out was impossible, which meant she had to hide the truth. Jimmy could never find out about her cancer.

Thinking about the bar reminded her that she had to work that night. Amanda started the car before backing slowly out of her spot, her mind on her predicament. The doctor had told her that surgery wasn't an option for her, at least not at that time. She needed to start chemotherapy as soon as possible, though, which meant they expected her at the hospital early the following morning. She would get a port followed by the first of the treatments. As long as she tolerated it well, she would be released that afternoon. It was to be the first of many.

Doctor Hunt had warned her that the treatments would be harsh, and she wouldn't be able to drive herself home. He'd talked as if he expected her to have someone available and willing to hold her hand as she went through the process. Amanda smiled bitterly. If only he knew.

Amanda had nobody. Even if she were foolish enough to tell Jimmy, he'd be the last person to comfort her. It was more likely she would find herself thrown out, with her belongings littering the grass in front of the double wide they lived in. Jimmy wouldn't stay single for long, though. While she was fighting for her life, his would go on as usual. And he wasn't the type of man to stay single for long.

It hurt, knowing she meant so little to the man she'd given the last six years of her life to. Had the situation been reversed, Amanda would have done everything in her power to support him. Where had it gone so wrong? Or had their relationship always been that way?

Jimmy was her first and only boyfriend. Amanda liked to call herself a late-bloomer, but if she was honest, the simple truth was there simply hadn't been any takers. She'd been twenty-three when she met Jimmy at the Red Ruby, the local country music bar she worked at in the small town of Nashoba. Fresh-faced and full of romantic notions, she was floored the first time he flirted with her, even more so when he asked her out on a date. Their relationship had progressed fairly quickly, and before she knew it she moved in with him. At the time, it was a dream come true.

But six years later the dream had turned into a nightmare. The first year or two she hadn't really minded his hateful comments or lack of consideration. She simply accepted him as he was, never judging him or attempting to change him. Caught up in the joys of experiencing love for the first time, she was able to easily explain it all away.

That had all changed in the prior year. After discovering Jimmy in bed with Bobbi, a petite, blonde divorcee from Nashoba, Amanda had been devastated. He'd stormed out in hot pursuit of the buxom Bobbie, while she had sunken to the floor in tears. It didn't escape her notice he'd left without even so much as an apology.

And in those dark hours that followed, she realized a simple but powerful truth. There wasn't much she wouldn't let him get away with because she was afraid—afraid he'd leave her and afraid she'd never find someone else. It wasn't as if the men had ever lined up at her door, even before Jimmy had come along.

Amanda was big. There wasn't anything on her that wasn't. Even her nose was big. Jimmy often made a point of reminding her of that. Her frame was solid, her thighs and hips in proportion with each other. She wore a size twenty-two comfortably, and she was taller than the average woman. According to Jimmy, she was the biggest woman he'd ever been with. It hadn't been a compliment.

Amanda's eyes welled up with a fresh wave of tears, a sob escaping her lips in the silence of the small car. She hated the woman she'd become, a woman so starved for love she'd settle for the cheating just to have someone in her life. She'd thought that one day he would change, but now she was out of time.

Jimmy can't find out about my disease. Nobody can, Amanda decided with resolve. Her treatments were every two weeks, and they'd always fall on a weekday. She'd talk with the doctor and schedule them for her off days. Surely, it would give her enough time to rest up before returning back to work.

Amanda pulled into the parking lot of the Red Ruby and gave herself a quick once over in the mirror of her car. After wiping away the tears, she inhaled deeply in an attempt to calm herself. Her cheeks were red, her eyes a little bloodshot, but it would have to do.

Braving the rain, she ran into the back entrance. Like always, she was right on time. Late afternoons were slow, which worked out perfectly for the shift change. Jean, the bar owner, usually worked days, but that didn't mean she wasn't there evenings, too. From the rumor mill, Amanda knew she'd all but lived at the Red Ruby for at least thirty years... and through two husbands. Now somewhere in her seventies, if not older, Jean still ran the bar with a firm hand and a sharp eye. She was widowed, her second husband having died a year before Amanda moved to Nashoba. Not a day passed by the woman couldn't be found somewhere within the building. The bar was Jean's life.

Walking down the empty hallway, Amanda quickly made her way to the front. Jean sat at the end of the bar, watching Jerry Springer as she drew deeply on a long cigarette. The woman smoked like a freight train, especially while watching talk shows.

Jean nodded at her before turning her attention back to the television. Amanda stowed her purse underneath the bar, quickly counting the patrons. It was just another typical weekday. The nights were a different story.

As the only bar in town, the Red Ruby served a wide variety of clientele. Everyone from bikers to traveling businessmen could often be found within its darkened depths, most of them looking for the same things—booze and sex. Many a marriage had been destroyed from a flirtation started within the bar, and as bartender it was Amanda's job to see nothing. She was there to serve drinks and work the cash register. Nothing more and nothing less.

"The boyfriend back in town?" Jean finally asked her, her wizened eyes narrowed on her face. Amanda jumped, surprised to see the other woman watching her so closely. Turning away from Jean she started to count the inventory, afraid of what the older woman might see in her face.

"No, he's out on the road," Amanda answered simply, hoping her short reply would end the conversation. Jerry was on a commercial break, which left Jean with several minutes to interrogate her, should she be of mind to. *God, I hate commercials.*

"Humph," Jean replied, tapping her cigarette against the ashtray. "I had a chance to marry a truck driver one time, but I turned him down flat. It's not good for a relationship to spend so much time apart, especially for a man. Men make mistakes when they get too much time away, you know what I mean? And those mistakes usually happen between the legs of some female that is only too happy to pick up the slack."

Do I ever know about a man's mistakes. Amanda kept her thoughts to herself, though. Her personal problems had no place on the job. Still Jean's words brought her busy hands to a halt as she considered them, and for the first time she wondered just how much the other woman knew about her personal life... And about Jimmy. Was it possible that she knew about his affair with Bobbi, or was Jean just making small talk?

Amanda shrugged it off. There was no way to know without outright asking, and she wouldn't be doing that anytime soon. "Has the delivery truck been through today?"

Jean waved her question away. "Yeah, the driver made an early run. I've already sorted it, though. Good thing, too. You look like you're coming down with something."

Without realizing it, Jean had just given her the perfect opening. "You know, I have been feeling a bit off today, but I'm sure I'll make it through my shift. It's probably just a summer cold. I'll sleep it off tomorrow." She wasn't scheduled to come in the following day.

The next several minutes passed by quietly. Despite her best intentions, Amanda's thoughts kept straying back to the doctor's words. She automatically assumed the chemotherapy would ultimately cure her, but what if she were wrong? She hadn't thought to ask about her life expectancy. At twenty-nine, the question just felt so wrong.

"I just don't get it," Jean rasped out, her husky voice revealing her years of smoking. She gestured toward the television mounted high on the wall. The flat screen revealed a middle-aged man with a teary eyed female seated next to him. Amanda shook her head in exasperation. The last thing she needed to watch was some jerk breaking another poor woman's heart. She had enough problems of her own.

Jean was oblivious. "This man is on here complaining because his girlfriend wants to marry him. I mean, so what? Isn't that the natural progression of things? You'd think it was some kind of crime or something. His attitude is just a bunch of garbage, if you ask me. What kind of world are we living in, when a woman is told it's wrong to want to marry the man she has feelings for?"

Amanda stopped and turned, politely listening as Jean talked. The other woman took a long sip of her ice water before clearing her throat and continuing, "Women have got it all wrong now. They give it up too soon, and the men don't respect them. And before you tell me I don't have a clue, let me tell you something. By the time I let my future husbands climb into my bed, I'd made them work for it. And you know what? By the time they left it the next morning, they were begging for me to marry them."

Jean grinned broadly as she winked at Amanda, her expression all-knowing. Amanda couldn't help but smile back, trying to picture the wrinkled woman as a seductress. It wasn't possible.

"Of course I outlived both of them, too," Jean added, stabbing her cigarette into the ashtray. "And I'm too old now to try for a third." She sighed despondently, her face settling into heavy lines as she frowned. "Thank God for this bar. If it weren't for it, I just might have withered away and died myself. Still, nothing can ever replace the love of a good man, or his strong, warm arms to hold you close throughout those late night hours."

Amanda wouldn't know. She might have lived with Jimmy for the last several years, but his arms had never been warm and they certainly hadn't held her. She turned back to the clipboard to finish up her inventory counts, her thoughts depressed. She might as well have been single for the last six years. There was only one thing worse than being alone, and it was feeling alone when you were supposed to be involved.

"You can talk to me, you know," Jean said quietly, her eyes meeting Amanda's in the mirror behind the cash register. "In all the years you've been here, I've never seen you really socialize. Everyone needs someone to confide it, at some point or another. Believe it or not, I've been told I'm a pretty good listener."

Her words surprised Amanda, but she wasn't

the type to share her problems... even if she might have wanted to. Careful to keep her expression blank, she turned her eyes away from Jean and grabbed up a clean rag to clean the bar. "Thanks for the offer," she replied casually, her voice even. "I appreciate it."

The rest of the night passed fairly quietly, but driving back home Amanda reflected on Jean's words and cried.

* * * * *

"Get stuck in any cars lately?" the younger werewolf quipped from the office as Ryker walked by, his buddies snickering at his words. Ryker glared at him as he flipped him the bird, not bothering to slow down. Dipshits like them were half the reason he'd decided to move outside of Wolf Town. Their never ending pranks, jokes, and outbursts were irritating as hell, and he'd finally had enough. If he hadn't moved he might have killed a few of them. Alexander wouldn't have appreciated the sentiment very much.

Ryker gripped his motorcycle helmet in his right hand, listening to it tap against his muscular thigh as he walked. He wasn't quite sure why he'd brought it in, unless subconsciously he'd wanted to club one of the other guardians with it. He relished the thought before turning his mind back to business.

Alexander had called him in for a meeting the hour before, and he hadn't sounded good. *What now?* Ryker could only speculate about the latest drama. When it came to problems, Wolf Town had seen more than their fair share... especially lately.

Sometimes he felt as if the werewolves as a whole were walking in a landmine, just waiting for the next explosion. It was bad times for supernatural creatures. The human's technological advances weren't their friend, and it seemed like every other human was on the hunt for a paranormal creature. *Damn television shows.* And now that the queen was breeding, anxiety levels were through the roof. It wasn't the best of times for any of them, although a pregnancy was always welcome news.

Ryker stopped to knock briskly on the king's office door, although he was sure the other man knew he was there. With his heavy, black biker boots, his footsteps had been loud as he'd walked down the hallway. Still, it was just good manners, and said manners were important to him.

"Enter," Alexander called out, his deep voice carrying easily through the wood. Ryker walked in, closing the door quietly behind him. To his surprise, they were alone. It wasn't the norm. When Alexander called a meeting, there were usually several wolves in attendance.

Alexander placed his pen down on his desk, standing up to shake hands with him. "Thanks for coming so quickly," he told Ryker, gesturing toward the leather chair across from him. "How are things coming along with your new home?"

"Very well, thank you," Ryker replied formally, sitting down stiffly into his seat. "I got completely moved in about a week ago." He'd never been much for small talk, it always left him uncomfortable, but put him into battle, and he was right in his element. There was little that meant more to Ryker than duty and honor; it was the code he lived by. But when it came to chit chat he was completely inept.

Alexander paused to stare at him, as if he were considering whether or not to pursue the topic. Both men were well aware of why Ryker had left. He was a loner, unaccustomed to the mischievousness of the other guardians he worked so closely with. They rubbed him the wrong way, often making him the brunt of their bad jokes and pranks. He could tolerate working with them, but just barely. He bared his fangs slightly, much to Alexander's obvious amusement. *Nobody could ever accuse me of being a team player.*

"Something bothering you?" the other man asked, steepling his fingers together in a pyramid as he leaned back in his seat. "Or are you thinking about your coworkers?" Alexander grinned. "Don't worry. Sometimes I fantasize about banging a few heads together myself."

"No, everything is fine," he assured him, changing the subject. "How can I assist you, Alexander?" Ryker pronounced his name in an accented voice, still not completely comfortable with the lack of formality. Their king had insisted on it, though.

The grin left Alexander's face, replaced with an expression of worry. Ryker's eyes widened just a fraction of an inch, but otherwise he was careful to conceal his reaction. Alexander had always been a fearless and bold leader, he'd never seen the other man look as discouraged as he did in that moment. Things were still bad at Wolf Town, apparently much worse than he'd thought.

Two months before, Wolf Town had almost experienced total annihilation by an alien race. For a time, Alexander had even considered sending their females and young away. They'd faced an enemy for which there was no known way to defeat. Thankfully, it hadn't turned into an all-out war, and the situation had been defused. But ever since then, something had been off at Wolf Town.

Maybe it was just the culmination of the events of the last six months, or maybe it was something more, but their carefree days were over with. An invisible cloud hung over their settlement, and their people couldn't seem to shake it. It was almost as if the werewolves were always on pins and needles, waiting for the other shoe to drop. *Will it never end?*

Alexander sighed heavily, lines temporarily bracketing the sides of his mouth. He narrowed his startlingly bright blue eyes at Ryker, his expression and voice firm when he said, "What I'm about to tell you does not leave this room, at least not at this point. Is that understood?"

"Of course," Ryker replied automatically, leaning forward in expectation. They both knew his word was good. It wouldn't be repeated.

Alexander raked a large hand through his

windswept hair before squeezing his fingers into a fist and slamming it down on his desk. "We're having a bit of a problem with our packs in Australia," he finally confessed, staring past Ryker to look out the window. "In fact, I would call it a major problem. The packs there have come together, and they've decided to challenge me for the role of king."

"What?" Ryker hissed out in disbelief, raking his own hand through his hair. "That's unbelievable. What the hell are they thinking? It's mutiny. They should all be punished."

"That's the thing," Alexander replied, his eyes moving back to Ryker's face. "It's not against pack law for them to challenge me. They are well within their rights to do so, especially if they think that I'm not strong enough to hold the position. Really, they don't even need an excuse. Hell, I'm surprised it hasn't happened before, although I'd thought better of our people than that. It couldn't have come at a worst time, though. God knows Carole Anne has been through enough since meeting me, and with her breeding, sometimes I wonder how much more she can take."

The thought seemed to disturb him greatly, but he managed to shake it off. "Naturally I will fight for my position. I'll even kill, if I'm forced into it. The world around us is dangerous enough, we have to be able to trust our own. Any traitors or troublemakers have to be weeded out. We have to remain united if we want to survive. There's safety in numbers. We can't have one pack, or one country of packs, ruining it for everyone."

"And this is where you come in, Ryker," Alexander continued, his eyes watching Ryker's face for his reaction. "I'm going to need a second, a werewolf that can and will fight to protect our way of life, should I fall. I won't ask Marrok, Connor, or even Ivan, all of them have mates, and it wouldn't be fair. So I'm asking you, but I don't want you to feel as if you have to accept this role. You can turn it down, and I won't think any less of you for it. It's an awful lot to ask of anyone."

Ryker exhaled, leaning back in his seat in disbelief. He didn't need to consider the request, naturally, he was only too happy to be second. Rather, the challenge itself had surprised him. Never, not once in his wildest dreams, would he have ever expected any werewolf to issue one. Why would they? Alexander had stepped into the role easily, it was his birthright.

"Of course," Ryker agreed, calmly. He wasn't the least bit concerned about the possible consequences, even less at the thought of losing his life. "It's highly unlikely I'll be needed, though. There are not many who haven't heard about your fighting skills. I almost pity the poor bastard."

Energy tingled beneath the surface of Ryker's skin. The wolf that lived within him anticipated the thought of such a dangerous fight. *He* wanted to join in. But that wouldn't happen unless Alexander fell, and that was the last thing Ryker wanted. He certainly wouldn't ever want to fill his shoes, it was way too much responsibility and commitment for a man like him. Ryker respected Alexander, but he didn't want to be him.

"Who is challenging you?" Truth be told, Ryker wasn't familiar with the process. It was the first time someone had tried to overthrow the king, at least in his lifetime. All werewolves were aware that it could happen, but actually doing it was a completely different story.

"Balor," Alexander replied, his expression tight. It was just a name, but it held a wealth of meaning. Ryker whistled, leaning back in his seat to think about it.

Balor was one of the largest wolves in the world, which was saying a lot considering that most of them were the size of horses when they shifted. Ryker didn't know the other wolf personally, but he'd seen him before. He had a reputation of being mean, and he was known as a troublemaker. Luckily, Balor seemed to prefer the isolation of the Australian outback, which was good for the rest of them. It kept him out of trouble.

Alexander held up a hand when Ryker opened his mouth to speak. "Before you ask, I don't know when this match will take place. I was officially notified by the Australian pack only yesterday, which is another reason why I don't plan to go public quite yet. I wanted to get my affairs in order and my second in place before telling anyone. Knowing Ivan as I do, he would have insisted on assisting me, and I couldn't let him do that. Now that I have your oath, though, at least that is no longer an issue. I don't want to reveal any of this any sooner than I have to, especially to Carole Anne. It's not an easy thing to tell your pregnant mate that you've got to leave—and might not be coming back."

At his words, they both fell silent. Alexander looked down at his papers while Ryker waited. It was a long time before either man spoke again.

Chapter 2

The next several days passed by quickly. Amanda's port surgery and subsequent chemotherapy had been a success, and although drowsy, she'd made the short drive from the hospital to the mobile home just fine. She had fallen asleep nearly immediately, too exhausted to worry about fixing herself a meal.

But the following day had been a nightmare. Upon waking, Amanda had found herself immediately nauseated, and it hadn't abated as the day progressed. An hour before her shift she'd forced herself to dress before running by the local drive-thru pharmacy. For once they hadn't been busy, and she was able to fill the prescription for nausea before going into work. The medication had helped immensely, but it had taken everything she had to remain on her feet throughout her shift.

Now it was Friday evening, and Amanda felt a great deal better. It was a good thing. The bar was always busy on Friday nights, which meant she wouldn't get home until late. At least she wouldn't be returning to an empty place. Her boyfriend was on his way back to Nashoba, he'd sent her a text earlier that afternoon. By the time she got off, Jimmy would be home but in bed. He always was an early riser.

"I'm heading out," Jean informed her, reaching beneath the bar for her purse. Her weathered cheeks held a tinge of pink that normally wasn't there. Amanda stared at her curiously. The older woman appeared to be embarrassed at her scrutiny. "Even if I do own the bar, I figure I deserve a night off, at least every now and then."

As Jean edged toward the end of the bar, Amanda could see why. An older gentleman waited patiently, his warm eyes locked onto the blushing female. He straightened up from the bar when she got close, an arm sliding out to escort her to the door. Amanda grinned widely. "I see," she replied, grabbing an empty bottle from the smooth wooden surface. "Enjoy your night."

Jean shot her an exasperated look before turning to leave with her date. Amanda watched them go. Funny, she hadn't realized that the older woman was interested in dating. *Will this one be proposing, too?* Chucking at the thought, and hoping that both of them survived the courtship, she waited for the waitress to give her the next drink order.

The remainder of the evening passed uneventfully. The early morning hours found Amanda unlocking the doors to her double wide, feeling along the wall in the dark for the light switch. During the week, she always left the lamp on. She hated returning to a dark place, but despite her numerous requests, Jimmy never remembered to leave it on. Or maybe he simply didn't want to. Either way, Amanda was too tired to try to figure it out.

Putting her purse down on the table, she walked down the hallway to their room, all but staggering in exhaustion. She'd only had one treatment so far, but the chemo affected her powerfully. Once again, she worried about what the future held for her. Would she be able keep her job? If just one exhausted her for days, how would she ever make it after five treatments? Ten? It was a depressing thought.

She reached out to turn the knob. To her surprise, it was locked tight. "What on earth?" Amanda muttered tiredly, trying it again. She hated to wake Jimmy, but she didn't have a choice. *He must have locked it by accident before he went to bed.*

Gently knocking on the door, she waited for her boyfriend to answer. When he didn't, Amanda called out, "Jimmy?" No answer. "The door is locked. Can you open it so I can come to bed?" Amanda hated the plaintive note in her voice, but there was no help for it. She was dead on her feet.

Several seconds passed as she stared at the door in disbelief. "Go away," he snarled suddenly, his voice harsh and rough. It was clear he'd been asleep, pretty deeply if his tone was any indication. Amanda frowned at the cruelness of his words, but he wasn't done yet. "I'm tired of you waking me up in the middle night. Sleep on the couch until you can get some better hours. You're not coming in here."

"Come on!" Amanda wasn't quiet when she tried the knob again. "This is ridiculous. All of my clothes are in there. How am I supposed to change?"

"Not my problem," Jimmy spat out. His voice was loud, even through the wood of the door. "From here on out, consider yourself warned. I'm locking this door at eleven every night, so change your hours or stow your shit somewhere else. I'm not playing, Amanda. I want my rest."

"It's not like I'm out on the town," she hissed, hitting the door with the palm of her hand. "I'm working, too. Did it ever occur to you that the hours might be hard on me, too?"

Jimmy didn't respond. She knew from past experience that continuing wouldn't do any good. When he was done talking, he was done. She'd just be wasting her time.

Amanda walked to the other side of the double-wide and into the guest bathroom, gently shutting the door behind her. "Unbelievable," she muttered to herself as she flipped on the light, leaning over the sink to take a look at herself in the mirror. With her dark circles and pale complexion, she looked as exhausted as she felt.

Luckily for her, she kept a spare toothbrush and some other necessities in their spare bathroom, although they never got used. Nobody ever spent the night, which was why there wasn't a bed set up in the guest bedroom. Sighing heavily, Amanda quickly brushed her teeth and washed her face before walking back to the living room. She refused to sleep on the floor, especially in a place that she mostly paid for. *The couch it is.*

Taking the two decorative pillows from each end, she placed them together and covered up with a throw that she kept on the back of the couch. The problems between them had escalated, whether she'd been aware of it or not. Not only did she have to worry about her job, but now she had to worry about her relationship, too. It was a heavy burden to carry. There was the very real possibility that she could find herself homeless and jobless. Even considering it would be terrifying for the healthiest person. For her, it was mind-blowing. Maybe even deadly.

What would happen to her if she got too sick to provide for herself? Amanda lowered her head down on the pillows, tears seeping out of the corners of her eyes. *God, I miss my parents so badly.* Had they still been alive, none of worries would have been an issue. Her parents would have taken care of her, just like she would have cared for them, had she only been given the opportunity.

And on that note, her exhausted body forced her to sleep.

* * * * *

The sound of a loud curse followed by a clanging pan woke Amanda the next morning. Sunlight immediately blinded her, streaming in from the uncovered windows. Amanda groaned, her neck in a crick from sleeping on it wrong. "Why did you open the curtains?" she asked Jimmy, her voice little more than a croak. "I've only had a few hours of sleep."

Jimmy grabbed another skillet from the cabinet, a charming smile on his face when he looked at her. With his dark hair and athletic build, he really was an attractive man. "I thought I'd make you some breakfast," he told her, his voice repentant. "You know, for being so grouchy last night."

Amanda groaned again as she buried her face in the pillow, wishing he hadn't felt the need to make amends. Even before the cancer, she'd never been a morning person. All she wanted to do was bury her face underneath her cover, but there was nothing she could do about it. He'd continue to pester her until she was up; it was just the way he was.

She threw the blanket to the side, coming unsteadily to her feet as she ignored Jimmy's smile of satisfaction. Making her way to the bathroom, Amanda took care of the necessities before walking back out to meet him. She wanted a shower badly, her clothing felt stiff and uncomfortable against her skin. It was pretty sad when someone had to be dirty and uncomfortable in their own home. She wasn't in a very charitable mood toward Jimmy, although he appeared to be the picture of contentment.

Jimmy sat at the kitchen table, smoking a cigarette as he turned on the television. Amanda looked between him and the empty stove, an expression of disbelief on her face. "I thought you were making breakfast?" she asked him, crossing her arms as she stood next to the sink. Nausea churned inside of her at the thought of food, but she had to eat. She'd already missed too many meals since her treatments had started.

He stopped turning the channels as he looked at her. "I was going to, but why ruin good food? You cook so much better, so I decided to let you do it." With a shrug, he resumed his channel surfing, quickly dismissing her from his mind.

Some apology. Amanda turned away from him without a sound, picking up the iron skillet that awaited her on the counter. Turning on the stove, she oiled it and placed it on the burner. "What do you want with your eggs?" she asked, her voice as flat as her mood.

"Some bacon and toast would be great," Jimmy replied absentmindedly, finally settling on a show. "By the way, I'm coming up to the bar tonight. The guys and I are going to have a few drinks and play some pool."

"Oh, do you want to drop me off today? You could stay till closing time, and I could ride home with you tonight." She hoped he would agree. It would be a nice change from her usual solitary drive.

"No, you better take your car," he replied regretfully but was it sincere? Amanda had her doubts. "I'm heading over to Frank's house in a few hours, and we're going to watch the game. I doubt I'll stay at the bar that late, and you know how I hate being up all night. I get enough of that on the road, you know what I mean?"

The next several minutes passed by quietly. Amanda filled his plate and carried it over to him, silently considering her own food choices. The doctors had warned her that she would likely lose quite a bit of weight due to nausea and appetite loss. She could see why. The very taste and smell of food seemed to have change. Would she ever regain her appetite again?

"Why are you wearing a turtleneck?" Jimmy asked her, pulling her from her thoughts. His upper lip curled up in distaste. "In case you haven't noticed, it's nearly a hundred degrees outside."

"Is it?" Amanda replied nonchalantly, casually shrugging. She turned away from him, keeping her expression as unconcerned as possible. The last thing she really needed was Jimmy asking questions. If he ever saw the port, their relationship would be over. He wasn't exactly known for his warm and fuzzy nature.

"Come to think of it, you look rather... unkempt," he continued, stopping only to finish chewing. "We all know you could stand to lose a few pounds, but that's no excuse for not trying to look your best. I hope you're not sick with something contagious. If you are, I can't be around you. I hate being on the road when I'm sick."

Amanda's fingers curled around the handle on the refrigerator door, her back to her boyfriend. *The insensitive prick*, she fumed silently. For the first time in their relationship, Amanda was truly fed up. What could she do about it, though? Inhaling deeply, she forced herself to say calmly, "I suppose that's what happens when you work a full shift and can't change your clothes." She didn't acknowledge his comments about her weight. Really, what was his problem? It wasn't as if she hadn't been heavy when he met her.

"About that," Jimmy retorted, in an

unapologetic manner. "I think you should move your stuff into the spare bedroom. I need to be able to sleep on the weekends, and I can't do that with you waking me up. You can do that this morning, you have plenty of time before your shift starts." He laid his fork down on the table before wiping his mouth with a paper towel.

Amanda turned around to stare at him in disbelief. He shot her a quick grin. "I've got to run," he informed her, coming to his feet. "You don't mind cleaning up, do you? I don't want to be late."

And with that, he turned around to walk out. Amanda looked around the kitchen, taking in the mess. *Yeah, some apology.*

* * * * *

Ryker stalked into the bar, his mood dark and dangerous. He didn't usually drink at bars full of humans, but after a week spent with his Neanderthal co-workers he was ready to make an exception.

The parking lot was packed, and the interior of the country western bar was, too. Nashoba was just a small town filled with ranchers and farmers, but it seemed they all had the same idea as him. He stopped in the doorway to survey the crowd, his arms crossed as he glared at anyone dumb enough to look in his direction.

Suddenly he smiled, which made a group of bikers decide to find another place to stand. In a bar as full as the Red Ruby, a fight was usually brewing somewhere. If he were real lucky, some tough guy asshole would decide to fuck with him. He was in the mood to crack a few skulls.

It was one of the reasons why Ryker generally avoided bars such as these. There was usually some prick that wanted to take on the biggest and baddest looking male in the bar, and that always described him. Said prick would approach him, usually with a few of his cronies in tow, and Ryker would have to set them down. In the past, he'd considered it a hindrance. But now? He just hoped someone decided to fuck with him.

Things back in Wolf Town were tense, at least between Ryker and the king. Alexander still hadn't officially announced the upcoming challenge, though they'd discussed it several more times. Neither one of them knew when it would happen, they just knew it would. It was likely the Australian wolves were garnering support before they officially set the date. There were steps they had to complete to make it formally valid. It didn't happen overnight.

That, combined with the irritating natures of his co-workers, was driving Ryker nuts. He couldn't understand it. He'd been in Wolf Town for years, and although they'd irritated him in the past, it had never been to the extent he was currently experiencing. *Maybe I've finally blown my lid*, he mused silently, mulling it over. After all, what man, especially a werewolf, liked to be made a fool of? And that was exactly what happened the night he'd been trapped in Orlando's car. He should have just ripped the small door off, but no. Instead, he'd come close to having a panic attack, and in the process, he'd shamed himself in front of all the other guardians. And the bastards wouldn't let him forget it. Even worse, one of them had even filmed it with his cell phone. God only knew how many had watched his humiliating experience. *Bastards.*

    He'd already moved clear out of Wolf Town, but that wasn't enough for him. Ryker was determined to avoid as much contact as possible, especially outside of his work. He might have to be around them during his guardian duties, but he didn't have to spend his free time with them. Which explained why he was spending his Saturday night at the Red Ruby, drinking with humans instead of werewolves. At least with humans he wasn't likely to kill anyone. *Not yet.*

    Spotting an empty bar stool, he cut through the crowd, determined to get to it before someone else did. The people in front of him parted like a warm knife through butter, which wasn't unusual. His don't-fuck-with-me persona came naturally, and most people reacted to it immediately. In other words, men avoided him but not the women. No, Ryker was used to women flocking to him, whether he wanted their attentions or not.

    He ignored all of them as he slid on the seat and waited for the bartender to take his order. It didn't take her long. Stopping in front of him, she wiped the back of her hand across her forehead tiredly before asking, "What can I get you?"

Ryker gave her his full attention, his breath hitching in his lungs. Tall and robust with thick hips and large breasts, the bartender was a true beauty. She reminded him of the women from his past, back in a time where curvy women were not only appreciated but sought after. *God, how I miss those days.*

For once in his life, Ryker was actually speechless. Their eyes connected and held, blue meeting blue in a heated exchange that all but floored him. Invisible electricity sizzled along his nerve endings, the sensation nearly burning him alive. His reaction to her was instantaneous. His shaft came alive in his jeans, thickening and pulsating underneath the suddenly too-tight material. Had they been alone he would have seduced her. Immediately.

Ryker inhaled automatically, his wolf searching for any signs that he'd finally found his mate. *Nothing.* She wasn't his mate, but her scent was odd. It held a thick, cloying scent that he hadn't encountered in a human before. He frowned. It almost reminded him of poison.

The attraction he felt toward her was powerful, certainly stronger than anything he'd ever experienced before. His control was all but shot, his wolf restless. The bartender blushed before finally breaking eye contact. She did it on the pretense of checking on the rest of the bar, but Ryker wasn't fooled. She felt the attraction, too. He was sure of it.

With a sigh, he remembered his reason for being there. "I'll have a draft," he told her, his voice naturally loud enough to be heard over the music. "Whatever you have on hand is fine but not light." Ryker hated the taste of light beer, and he certainly didn't have to worry about his weight. The wolf, combined with his daily physical activities, kept his body in prime condition.

"S-sure," the bartender replied, turning to grab a mug from the counter behind her.

In her jeans and turtleneck every curve was revealed, and the back view certainly didn't disappoint. His mind went straight to the gutter. Ryker's fingers curled up as he imagined locking onto her lush hips to hold her in place for his thrusts. *She's a lusty one*, he decided immediately. Most women of her proportions were. It was as if their bodies were created for the pleasures that could be found in bed. He nearly groaned as he imagined her curves pressed up against the hard lines of his body. With a woman built like her, he could give her everything he had, and she'd only crave more. Nothing turned a man on faster than a woman that couldn't get enough of what he had to offer. His shaft jerked hard at the thought. When it came to him, he had more than enough to see her satisfied.

It's too bad she isn't mine, Ryker mused silently. He was immediately surprised by the thought. *Since when do I want a mate?* He puzzled it out for a long moment, staring at her as she filled his mug. No, he ought to be thanking God she wasn't his. With the upcoming challenge, it wasn't the time for an unmated wolf to meet his fated one. Especially considering the fact there was no guarantee he'd be alive to enjoy her.

Maybe the last few months were affecting him more than he'd realized. Ryker ran a hand through his hair before exhaling deeply. *Am I hitting some type of werewolf midlife crisis?* First, he'd left Wolf Town, and now he was envisioning a mate. What next? Bird watching? Board games? Retirement homes?

She sat his mug down on a coaster before taking the twenty he held out. "Just keep the change," he told her, pleased at the flash of surprise and appreciation deep within her blue eyes. With her doll-like features and plump lips, the woman really was a beauty. *A natural beauty*, he corrected himself, taking in her bare mouth and eyelids. If she wore any make up at all, it was minimal.

"Thank you," she replied, her eyes darting in every direction but his. *Interesting.* He wasn't used to women like her. She was attracted, he could scent her interest, but instead of making a play for him she was pulling away. Was she shy? It didn't seem likely, especially considering where she worked, but it was the only explanation he could come up with.

Ryker wasn't used to shy, inexperienced women. Female werewolves were bold and fearless. If they saw a male they desired, they had no issues with making it known. A male werewolf could scent arousal. If they were unmated, they were quite likely to reciprocate. Sex was as natural to them as eating or sleeping, only much more pleasurable. It wasn't until they met their mates that it became significant. Once mated, a werewolf lost any interest in anyone besides their partner. It was life-changing, and an event that all of them looked forward to. Finding that one person that fate created specifically just for you was pretty powerful, even to someone as jaded as Ryker. He just hadn't found her yet.

The bartender had a touch-me-not air that Ryker found extremely attractive. Most women would have worn as little as possible in her position, eager to use their bodies to aid their tips. Not this woman, though. She was completely covered from the neck down.

His eyes narrowed on her turtleneck. It was unusual to see one at that time of year. Why would the female wear such a stifling shirt in such hot weather? The Missouri summers were known to drag on, even that late in the season. If she were modest, she took it to a level he hadn't seen before. At least not outside of the Amish community that bordered Nashoba.

Just as he was about to look away, he noticed it. High on her shoulder was a small but definite bump. *What the hell?* His eyes flashed back to her face, but she was unaware of his scrutiny. Instead of watching him, her eyes were trained on the pool room, a look of distress on her pretty features.

Eager to see what had caught her attention, Ryker turned, too.

Chapter 3

Holy shit, Amanda thought to herself as she forced her eyes away from the stud that sat at the bar. He was incredibly hot, made more so by the fact that he didn't appear to be conceited by it. And his large tip had definitely bolstered her spirits. She just wished all of her customers were as considerate.

He was easily one of the tallest men she'd ever seen—if not the tallest. Even seated on the stool, he was as tall as she was standing. With his black hair and vivid blue eyes, he was a total heart breaker. It wouldn't take long for one of the single women in the bar to approach him, already he was garnering their glances.

Jimmy had arrived a half-hour before, but with the exception of ordering some beers he'd all but ignored her. She looked back into the pool room, spotting him easily through the smoke and the darkened lights and frowned. It would appear that the guys weren't playing alone, if the blonde-haired bimbo wrapped around her boyfriend was any indication.

Amanda was furious. She wanted to march back there and sock the woman that had the nerve to touch her man, but something held her back. As she watched, Jimmy took a long swig from the bottle before sending the woman next to him a long, seductive smile. *The bastard was encouraging her,* Amanda realized dimly, her thoughts moving in slow motion. He had so little respect for her and their relationship that he would flirt with another woman, even right there in the place where she worked.

"Someone you know?" the man in front of her asked, his voice a sexy drawl. Startled, her eyes darted to his face, having momentarily forgotten his presence. He turned and gave Jimmy one last glance before shrugging dismissively. "Personally, I don't see much back there that's even worth watching."

"My boyfriend," Amanda managed to croak out before blushing again. Although she didn't know the man in front of her, she was humiliated beyond belief.

"Aha," the stranger replied, finishing his draft. "Let me guess, he's the one with the blonde?"

Amanda nodded before refilling his mug. Much to her surprise, he handed her another twenty. "You know the drill."

She gaped at him. "Are you sure?" she asked him, hating to take so much. "Really, getting you a draft isn't any trouble. It's definitely not worth this much. I feel bad, taking such a large tip from you."

"Don't," he replied, brushing away her words. "I'm giving it to you, aren't I? It's not as if you're taking it from me. Do me a favor, though. Don't spend it on that piece of trash back there. Something tells me you're getting the short end of the stick, at least when it comes to him."

A customer from down the bar called for her, holding his mug up in the air impatiently. Amanda turned away from the dark-haired man without answering, hurrying to wait on her next customer. She didn't know what to make of their conversation, and she was still furious with Jimmy. Day by day, he was making it harder for her to stay with him, and he seemed hell-bent on destroying her self-esteem in the process.

And there were no answers to be found in the next few hours. The crowd only increased, much to Jean's delight. Climbing off of her perch, she helped Amanda behind the bar. Even the waitresses were run ragged, and it didn't take long until Amanda all but forgot about Jimmy. With the press of bodies, she wasn't able to see him anyhow.

The dark-haired stranger remained, but judging from the women that quickly left his side he wasn't very social. For some odd reason, Amanda approved. Whatever he was looking for, it wasn't a one-night stand. As busy as she was she didn't have the chance to wait on him again, but Jean kept his mug full. Amanda idly wondered if he tipped the older woman as well as he had her. Her lips curved up slightly in a rueful grin. If so, it was likely she'd never get the chance to wait on him again.

Lost in her thoughts, Amanda didn't immediately see the customer at the bar. He knew it, and it enraged him. "Excuse me, you fat twat," he roared, waving his empty mug about wildly. "I said I want a refill. Has the fat filled your ears or something? Get me a damned drink."

He smirked at the people on each side of him.

Some of them sent him approving glances, while others stared at Amanda with a snide expression on their faces. She immediately blushed, embarrassed by his words, and the attention he caused. There were a few laughs, which only humiliated her further.

Her eyes met Jean's in question, but she was certain she already knew the answer. The older woman moved her hand across the front of her throat, a firm expression on her face. The irate customer wouldn't be served anymore drinks that night, at least not at the Red Ruby. Unfortunately, it was up to Amanda to deliver the news. It wouldn't be pretty.

Resigning herself to a scene, she looked back at the hateful male that watched her. "You're cut off," she informed him, her voice calm despite her embarrassment. "I can get you a pop, coffee, or water, but I won't be able to serve you anything alcoholic."

Her drunken customer stared back at her silently, rage simmering in his eyes. He looked to be somewhere near thirty, well past the age where he should have been old enough to handle his alcohol. Every conversation in the bar had ceased as the customers stopped to watch the newest drama unfold. *Where is Jimmy, and why isn't he helping me?* The bar wasn't *that* big. With everyone's attention focused on her, she didn't see how he could have missed it. Amanda grabbed a towel and started to clean the bar, ignoring all of them in an attempt to diffuse the situation.

The irate customer wouldn't let it go.

"Unbelievable," he finally said. He looked at the people next to him as he scoffed, "This fat bitch thinks to deny me—a paying customer. Who the hell does she think she is?" he continued, his tone filled with disgust.

Amanda continued to wipe the bar, her lips pressed in a thin line. She was filled with tension over the confrontation, hating every moment of it. He grabbed onto her arm painfully, his fingers digging into her skin. "Fat bitches like you are second-class citizens," he informed her angrily. "Or haven't you learned that? No? I'm going to teach you a lesson, one you're not likely to forget."

As if in slow motion he pulled his arm back while his fingers clenched into a fist. Amanda tried to yank away from him, but he wouldn't let her. His grip was unbreakable. He was going to punch her straight in her face, and there wasn't anyone who cared enough to stop him.

Or so she thought. In the blink of an eye, he was lifted clear off his feet from behind as his fingers were yanked away from her arm. Those seated next to him scrambled off their stools, their expressions filled with a mixture of fear and anticipation. The handsome stranger held the drunken customer up in the air, his expression furious.

He dropped the inebriated man on the ground before flipping him over to pick him back up by the front of his shirt. "Outside, now," he bit out, his expression deadly. No other words were needed, it was clear to everyone what his intentions were.

"I'm sorry," the shorter male screamed, a panicked expression on his face. "I wouldn't have really hit her. She just pissed me off."

"Bullshit," her rescuer proclaimed, his deep voice as cold as ice. "You sanctimonious little shit. Where the hell do you ever get off thinking you're better than anyone else—you, a man that would go around hitting on women? If it's a fight you're looking for, I'm more than happy to oblige you. I'm going to drag your sorry ass out through those doors and beat the hell out of you, and then we'll talk about apologies later—if you're even able to."

"No," he screamed out, his eyes suddenly clear and sober. "You're too big, it wouldn't be fair. You'd murder me with just one punch."

"And what do you think your fist would have done to her?" He shook the other man with one hand effortlessly, much to Amanda's surprise. His expression was calm, but his eyes were a different story. He was unbelievably angry, and within those blue depths, Amanda saw death.

"Throw his ass out," Jean said grimly, moving to stand next to them. Her expression was angrier than Amanda had ever seen it. The older woman jabbed her finger into the drunken male's chest as she added, "Don't you ever let me see your face in this bar again. I don't even want to see you in my parking lot. If I do, I'm calling the police. I don't have any patience for pricks like you, and neither does the sheriff. Now get the hell out of my bar before I change my mind and have you locked up."

With a toss of his powerful hand, the stranger released him. The other man fell in the floor before quickly coming back to his feet. Without another word, he ran for the door as if he feared pursuit. It would be a miracle if he made it home without wetting his pants.

The conversations resumed. The drama was over, and the patrons were eager to get back to their drinking and socializing. A line formed at the bar. Several minutes went by before she realized her savior was gone. It left her feeling glum. She hadn't even got the chance to ask him his name.

*****

The next several weeks passed by quietly. Amanda completed her second and then third chemotherapy treatment. She'd become a master at hiding the symptoms in public, and Jimmy was home so rarely she found it easy enough to keep up the pretense of feeling good. He'd opted to work the weekends from two of the previous four weeks, which left her with plenty of alone time. Instead of missing him, she'd only felt relief at his absence. It didn't bode well for their future together, should they have the possibility of having one.

Her doctor hadn't made her any promises, but he was optimistic that with treatment they could extend her life by several years. New options were becoming available all the time, or so he'd said. The important thing was staying alive long enough to possibly try one of them.

The side effects were more apparent with each visit. She'd started to lose her hair by the handfuls, often finding it in the shower drain or on her pillow. No longer could she conceal it, which had prompted her visit to a wig shop. With a little assistance from the clerk, she'd selected one that was flattering. Blonde and styled in big, loose curls, she hoped it looked natural enough to pass off as her own.

Jimmy had texted her earlier in the day, informing her he'd be home for the weekend. This time, Amanda was better prepared for his return. The week before she'd been lucky enough to find a nearly new twin-sized bed at the local thrift store. It had taken her awhile, but she'd eventually got it set up in the guest bedroom. She'd also moved her stuff out of the master bedroom, without complaint.

Truth be told, she was relieved to have her own room. Jimmy had hurt her deeply by changing their sleeping arrangements, and she was tired of his constant rejections and lack of consideration. Had she fallen out of love with him, or was she simply too exhausted and ill to be concerned? For the past year, their sex life had been all but non-existent. In fact, she couldn't even remember the last time they'd been intimate. Jimmy wasn't the type to go without. It wouldn't surprise her at all to discover he was cheating again. *Once a cheater, always a cheater.*

It was late Friday evening, and she was due at

work. Getting out of the car she patted the wig down on her head, hoping that it stayed in place. It felt weird, but the clerk had assured her she'd grow use to it. She fought the urge to scratch at her scalp. Maybe it was her nerves, or maybe it was the material, but the darn thing itched. After Jimmy went back out on the road, she planned on cutting off the rest of her natural hair. Hopefully, that would help.

Amanda took her time walking to the back entrance. Much to her dismay, she felt winded by the time she reached it. Her most recent treatment had affected her the most, and she was having a hard time bouncing back from it. Stiffening her slouching shoulders, she forced herself to walk in with purpose, nearly running over Jean in the process.

"I'm so sorry," Amanda said, her cheeks growing warm. "I should have been watching where I was going."

"Good grief," Jean muttered, her eyes lingering on Amanda's face. They didn't miss anything. She gently grasped her arm before tugging at it. "You don't look so well. Let's go in my office," she suggested kindly, her face concerned. "Are you ill?"

Amanda looked down the hallway, hesitant to allow the other woman to get too close. She felt vulnerable, her emotions close to the surface. What if she revealed too much and lost her job? "The bar will be fine," Jean added, believing her to be concerned about the customers. "We've only got a few regulars, and they just got fresh drinks."

"All right," Amanda agreed, completely deflated. She let Jean lead her to a chair, watching silently as the other woman found her own seat. "I'm okay," she said hesitantly. "I just need to pay more attention."

"No, you're not okay," the other woman disagreed sternly, her expression allowing no argument. "And I can't pretend you are anymore. Over the last several weeks I've watched you change from a healthy young woman to one that can barely stand. You've lost a great deal of weight, you've got deep circles underneath your eyes, and now you're wearing a wig. If I had to guess, I would say you have cancer."

Amanda stared back at Jean, losing control over her emotions by the second. For some reason she was reminded of her mother, although physically there wasn't much resemblance. Her mother had been quite a bit younger than Jean when she died, sealing Amanda's recollections of her appearance forever. *How I miss her.*

Maybe it was the concern she saw in the other woman's eyes, or maybe it was just the stress of dealing with a traumatic illness by herself, but regardless of the reason Amanda couldn't stop her sob. A second later, she found herself in a full-blown crying jag as hot tears raced down her face.

Jean got up to grab some tissues before moving her chair closer to hers. She handed them to Amanda before gently patting her on the back. "There now," she crooned to the younger woman. "Whatever it is you can trust me. I want you to know this."

"Is my illness that obvious?" Amanda asked quietly, her hand checking her wig. "I'd hoped it wouldn't be."

"Not at all," Jean reassured her. "You don't get to be my age without having the ability to recognize a wig, though. I doubt anyone else will ever notice, especially here in the bar. Most of them are too drunk to even hit the toilet when they piss, much less see someone's hair clearly."

"I can't lose my job," Amanda said quietly, her voice thick with emotion. Already, her tears were slowing. She hated crying, but maybe she'd needed to. The last several weeks had been horrible.

Jean didn't immediately reply. Instead, she watched Amanda with a sad expression on her gently-lined face, her eyes shadowed with pain. After a moment, she cleared her throat. "Of course not, dear," she reassured her, lowering herself back down into her chair. "You've been the best bartender I've ever had. Why on earth would I want to lose you?"

"You might not feel that way after you hear what I have to say," Amanda replied, her voice low. Unable to stand the pity in Jean's eyes, she looked away. "I have an advanced form of pancreatic cancer. It was just confirmed about five weeks ago, and I started treatment for it the next day. I only have to do it every other week. I thought I was managing the side effects pretty well, at least until now. This last treatment was pretty rough. It seemed to take more out of me than the previous ones."

"I see," Jean said, solemnly. "Does Jimmy know?"

It was the question Amanda dreaded the most. "No. And he can't know."

At her words, Jean looked puzzled. "Why not? You can't keep it a secret forever, Amanda. Chemotherapy is not something to play with. You're going to need someone to help as you progress through it. Whether you want to or not, you have to tell him. I mean, he is your boyfriend."

"You don't understand," Amanda choked out, horrified at the thought. She grabbed Jean's hands, silently pleading for the other woman to comprehend her predicament. "Our relationship is not very good right now. Jimmy isn't the type of man who likes to be tied down, especially with someone who can't pay her share of the bills. It wouldn't be fair to him."

"Not fair to him?" Jean's eyes flashed with anger. "What about you? How is any of this fair to you? It's not like you asked for cancer. Besides, I'm sure he makes quite a bit of money, surely more than enough to cover the household bills."

"We're not married, though."

Jean snorted. "So what? You're his girlfriend, and the woman he's lived with for six years. You've been his wife in every way except for name. He has a responsibility to you, whether he realizes it or not."

If only her words were true, but Amanda knew he wouldn't see it that way. It might have taken years, not to mention a terminal illness, but she was finally starting to see her relationship for what it really was. It wasn't pretty. She'd always wondered why Jimmy didn't want to marry her, but she'd never let herself think on it for very long. Maybe it was time she finally faced it.

"He's not faithful to me," Amanda said out loud, her voice filled with the pain of finally acknowledging her disastrous relationship. "And he doesn't love me, at least not in the way that a man should love a woman. He doesn't even want me sleeping in the same bed with him, which is why I sleep in the guest room. I can't leave him, though. If I leave him, I have nowhere to go, and I can't be homeless, especially now."

"Oh, no," Jean murmured sympathetically, patting her hand. "I didn't realize it was that bad. Why on earth did you ever stay with him? Believe it or not, he actually did you a favor by not marrying you. You could have left him at anytime and found someone better."

"Could I have?" Amanda stared at Jean blindly, a bittersweet smile playing about her lips. "I don't think so. I haven't exactly seen the men lining up, if you know what I mean."

"Then you haven't seen what I have." Realizing that Amanda no longer needed the tissues, she held out a small trash can for her to toss them in. "I've seen several men attempt to approach you, but you've always shut them down. I used to think it was because of your involvement with Jimmy, but now I realize that you never even recognized it for what it was. It's almost as if you've erected some type of invisible shield. You would have never welcomed their advances, and the men knew it. So they gave up before ever even trying. They knew that no matter what they did, you wouldn't be interested."

Amanda processed her words, her mind racing. It was a far-fetched, but there was also truth to it. Maybe she had erected a wall, one created from her belief that she was unattractive. Her lack of self-confidence wasn't unfounded, though. She'd had plenty of help along the way, originating from men that loved to insult any imperfection. In her case, it always came back to her weight.

Once she'd found Jimmy, she settled. In the beginning, she wouldn't have been interested in anyone else due to her feelings for him. But after he cheated, she'd pretty much given up on love. Emotionally, Amanda was tapped out. Starting a new relationship and potentially experiencing the same was more than she could have handled.

"Whether or not you decide to tell Jimmy, I want you to know you'll always have a job here. If it gets to be too much, just let me know. I've been thinking about adding on a part-time bartender anyhow. I can always cut your hours back."

Amanda smiled at her in appreciation. Jean was taking it much better than she'd expected. She was lucky to have such an understanding boss. "Thanks for the offer, but I really need the money. God only knows how much this is going to cost, and I don't have any insurance."

Jean frowned, but she didn't comment on it. Instead, she just looked sad. "What is your prognosis?" she finally asked quietly.

"Not very good." Saying it out loud just made it that more real. She wasn't strong enough to face her mortality. Not yet. "My doctor is on a mission to do everything he can to keep me alive. He believes that one day there will be a more effective treatment for pancreatic cancer, but it's not quite here yet."

"The chemo is rather debilitating, isn't it?" Jean asked, inhaling deeply. "I lost a daughter to breast cancer twenty years ago. She was about your age when she was diagnosed. In those days, a young woman with breast cancer was virtually unheard of. And even if a doctor did manage to diagnose them in time, the treatments weren't as good as they are now."

Her eyes were bright with tears. Jean valiantly tried to blink them away before they could slide down her cheeks, but she wasn't quite successful. "Julie was a late bloomer in everything, or so it seemed. At twenty-nine, she'd just gotten engaged, and Tom was a wonderful man. The future seemed bright for her, but one day her doctor discovered a lump during her annual physical. After that, it all went downhill."

"I'm so sorry to hear that, Jean," Amanda said sincerely. She knew the older woman had a few grown children, but she'd never seen them. They lived in another state.

Jean nodded. "I love all my children equally, but Julie was the baby. She's the one who decided to remain here in Missouri, and she still lived with me. At first, we were optimistic. With the exception of the cancer, Julie was a very healthy woman. The doctors went in and removed it, and she started chemotherapy and radiation. But it was too much for her."

She wearily sighed, suddenly looking much older than she had. "I watched her go from this bright, vivacious female to a former shell of herself. Her body couldn't overcome the cancer eating away at it, or the treatments that were supposed to help. She suffered quite badly, and I felt powerless to make it stop. It's a very horrible feeling, standing by and watching someone you love dying, right in front of your very eyes."

Jean stood up to push her chair back to her desk. "I want you to promise me that you'll come to me if you need to. I don't care if it's just because you need to talk, or even if you need a place to stay. Nobody should have to go through something like this alone."

Amanda nodded, her thoughts heavy as she came to her feet.

Chapter 4

Amanda drove home quickly that night, eager to seek out her bed. Despite the lateness of the hour, it wasn't as dark as it usually was. The moon was full, casting its light over the thick woods and forests she had to pass.

Her thoughts turned to the handsome man that had rescued her. She hadn't seen him since that night, and Jean hadn't mentioned him again. He was probably just a traveler, a person passing through. It wasn't likely that she'd see him again, but she couldn't get him out of her mind. He'd stood up for in a way that nobody else ever had. She hated that he'd left before she could thank him.

Pulling up in the driveway, she was surprised to see the mobile home ablaze with lights. Had Jimmy waited up for her? She smiled at the thought. In the early days of their relationship, he'd always made a habit of doing just that when he was home on the weekends. He hadn't done it in years. Maybe their relationship wasn't as doomed as she believed. Despite their troubles Amanda was willing to meet him halfway, if he'd only show the effort.

Turning off the headlights, she climbed out of the car and walked up the steps that led to the front door. Once she was on the deck, the porch light came on. Jimmy stepped outside. Amanda immediately tensed at the expression on his face, the smile leaving her own. He didn't look happy.

Closing the front door behind him, he stood in front of it with his arms crossed. "I don't know how else to tell you this, Amanda, so I'm just going to say it. We're done."

"What?" Amanda asked in disbelief, shaking her head in puzzlement.

Jimmy cleared his throat. "We're done. Finished. Our relationship, if you even want to call it that, is over." He spoke each word slowly, as if she were incapable of comprehending them. She didn't appreciate his mocking gesture.

Amanda went to move past him, but he blocked her off. "I'm not letting you in. I've already packed up your shit," he informed her, gesturing to a pile on the ground she hadn't noticed. "Everything that's yours is here. You need to take it and leave. Now."

"You can't just throw me out in the middle of the night," she told him, completely stunned by the turn of events. "It's cruel and mean. I'll sleep here tonight and leave in the morning."

Once again she made to move past him, but this time he grabbed her arm and slapped her across her cheek. "I said no," he roared, the veins in his throat sticking out. "Damn, don't you have any pride? I tried to be nice, but apparently you can't this through your thick skull. I. Don't. Want. You."

He shoved her back, an expression of distaste on his face. "I'm not sexually attracted to you, and God only knows why I let it get this far. I mean, look at you," he gestured at her frame, his fingers waving up and down. "Apparently, you've lost some weight, but even that hasn't helped. You look like shit. I'm sorry, I can't even trick my dick into getting hard for you. It's over."

The front door opened again, this time revealing a petite, young blonde in the doorway. Immediately, Amanda recognized her. It was the woman from the bar, the one who had hung all over Jimmy the last time he'd been in to play pool. Wearing nothing but one of Jimmy's shirts, she'd clearly made herself at home. *In my home.*

"Is everything okay?" she asked Jimmy, staring at Amanda with the same look of disdain that Jimmy wore on his own face. "I miss you. Come back to bed." Her throaty tone left no doubt to her meaning.

"I'm on my way," he replied to her, his eyes never leaving Amanda's face. "Make sure you're naked when I get there," he added cruelly. "I can't get enough of looking at that fit, lean body of yours."

The woman giggled in delight before closing the door.

"As far as I'm concerned my conversation with you is over," he told Amanda, turning around to go inside. "And make sure to change your address. I'm sending back anything that comes here for you, so don't even think about swinging by to pick up your mail. I don't want to see you here. Ever. After tonight, there is no reason for you to return. I can't believe I wasted six years on you. You're pathetic."

Amanda walked down the steps, angrier than she could ever recall being. Her cheek felt swollen, her emotions shredded, but she wouldn't give Jimmy the satisfaction of seeing her cry. She quickly collected her pitifully small pile of belongings. By the time she was done, her legs were shaking from exhaustion.

But she didn't let herself rest. Amanda started up the car and backed out, watching as Jimmy shut the door. She hadn't missed the expression on his face. The bastard was relieved to see her leaving.

She drove down the lonely, deserted road, with no clear destination in mind.

* * * * *

Ryker ran through the woods, enjoying the feel of the moon on his body. As a werewolf, he lived for nights like these. There was nothing quite like it.

He was nearing the end of his run, having been out for hours. Rural Missouri was the perfect spot for a werewolf on the night of the full moon. He wasn't tired, but his wolf was satisfied. It had been a good evening.

Miles of woods surrounded the two-story home he'd purchased, the isolation suiting him well. His nearest neighbor was nearly a mile away, far enough that he'd never felt obligated to even introduce himself. The lack of civilization afforded him freedom and safety, something he wouldn't have found in the more populated areas of the world.

The same could be said for Wolf Town, but Ryker preferred his current arrangement. Something had changed within him over the last few months, leaving him with a desire for solitude. He'd found it in the brick home and two-hundred acres he'd purchased, but he still felt empty. *Lonely.*

Does my wolf crave his mate? Ryker asked himself, for perhaps the hundredth time. Over the last several weeks, he'd begun to wonder. If so, why now? He'd spent hundreds of years without her and been fine, but now he was haunted by the ghost of the mate he'd yet to meet. Nothing seemed to ease it.

As he jumped over a fallen log a man's angry voice reached him, followed by the lower sound of a woman's voice. Ryker came to a halt, his ears perked up as he strained to hear more. Their voices were out of place in the quiet peacefulness of the woods. After a brief hesitation, he decided to investigate.

His furry feet moved silently across the leaves and grass, and it didn't take him long to find them. Concealing his head within the thick foliage from some bushes, he watched the man and the woman across the small road, easily hearing their conversation despite the distance.

His eyes widened when he recognized the feminine form. It was her, the woman from the bar, the one that had haunted his dreams. She'd changed in the four weeks since he'd last seen her, her voluptuous form not quite as solid as he remembered it. Even though it was dark, Ryker was able to see her clearly. It was one of the many benefits of being a werewolf.

She looked tired, her shoulders drooping as if

she bore the weight of the world on them. He snarled as he turned his attention to the man. *The boyfriend.* Ryker remembered him well. He was a coward, a man undeserving of the gentle beauty who stood in front of him.

Are they fighting? It certainly seemed to be the case. Ryker hadn't realized she lived so close to him, but now he could easily detect her scent all over the property. *They live here together,* he realized belatedly, surprisingly angered by the thought. His eyes swept over the bags on the grass. Or maybe not—at least not anymore.

When the man raised his hand and slapped her, Ryker saw red. He rose up on all fours, his body tensing to leap across the paved road. He'd tear him from limb to limb, regardless of the consequences. Nobody would hit her, not while he was there to stop it.

The door opened, a woman smirking as she watched the two in front of her. Ryker recognized her, too, but not because of her beauty. In that moment, he summed up the situation.

With his fur bristling, he watched the bartender collect her belongings. In the glow of the moonlight her face looked tired, her movements unsteady. Ryker's anger only increased, but really, the woman was better off without her cowardly boyfriend. He'd let her down that night in the Red Ruby, choosing to remain with his cronies and sluts while his girlfriend had been insulted and humiliated. And now, he'd just struck her. Was it the first time, or was it just one of many? Ryker didn't know, but he would take retribution.

Finally, she was done. Her small car was old and beaten up, Ryker marveled at how it even still worked. In its condition, he wouldn't have expected for it to be drivable.

Despite the lateness of the hour, he decided to follow her as she moved slowly down the road. He couldn't explain why he was so interested, but something about her called to him. She was lonely, too; he'd seen it in her pain-filled eyes that night at the bar. How could a female have a man but be so vulnerable? There was something mysterious and intriguing about her, and the wolf inside of him was curious to discover her secrets.

Ryker was easily able to keep up with the speed she drove. In wolf form, he was extremely fast. Even if he lost sight of her though, he could still track her—and he would. He'd been blessed with an exceptional ability to scent. There wasn't anywhere she could go that he couldn't find her.

Although pleasant, her scent had an extra repugnant element that didn't belong. It was blended heavily with her pheromones, so clearly it wasn't a perfume. It troubled him. Even so, Ryker couldn't help but inhale her scent deeply as pleasure spread throughout his body. She reminded him of coconut, suntan oil, and tropical islands. She was like a pina colada. Just breathing her in was a heady experience.

A mile passed and then another. She slowed down and turned onto a bumpy dirt road before carefully pressing on the accelerator. Ryker knew the road well. Eventually, it would end at a clearing by a lake, an area that some used as a campground.

Does she plan on spending the night in her car, all alone and in the woods? It appeared so, but it didn't make sense to him. Surely she had somewhere else to stay, or friends or family who would be willing to take her in. Between the heat and the mosquitoes, she wouldn't find it to be a pleasant stay, especially if she remained in the small car she was in. Ryker shuddered. Thanks to Orlando, he now had a serious aversion to small vehicles.

The lights from the car slashed across the clearing, revealing it to be completely vacant. Ryker wasn't surprised. Camping in extreme heat was very unpleasant, especially when you were spending your time in a tent—or a car.

The woman drew to a halt and cut off her engine, leaving the area in complete darkness. She rolled down her windows, but she didn't attempt to get out. Ryker watched her curiously, waiting for her next move.

But as he stared she leaned over the steering wheel and started to cry, her harsh sobs stabbing into him like a knife. He couldn't take it. Without thinking of the consequences, he shifted before stepping out from behind the trees.

* * * * *

Amanda jerked her head up from the steering wheel when someone cleared their throat, immediately terrified at the sound. She should have known better than to head out to the woods, but where else could she stay? From the corner of her eye, she caught movement. Turning her head, her terror changed to shock as her jaw gaped open. There in front of her stood the very man who had haunted her thoughts since the night he rescued her. And if that wasn't fantastical enough, he was completely nude.

Moonlight kissed his body, as if it, too, found him too irresistible to ignore. He advanced upon her, his body tall and proud as if he were in his element. Amanda gulped hard. In the mixture of darkness and light, his blue eyes appeared to glow. He had to be a delusion, a fantasy created from her distress and illness. There was no other explanation.

Her eyes locked onto the area between his legs, her heart speeding up when she saw it growing. Fantasy or not, the man was *seriously* endowed. She'd never seen such a meaty cock. Clearly, Jimmy was lacking in that department.

Fully erect, his shaft extended away from his body at an angle, almost as if it were begging to be touched. *He has to have some serious muscle power to lift something like that.* As thick as a water bottle, he was at least ten inches long, with large, round testicles to frame him.

He stopped a few feet away from her window, much to her regret. *What would I have done, had he come closer?* From where she was sitting, her face was on eye level with the area between his muscular thighs.

She should be scared, but Amanda was only fascinated. She was captivated by the moonlight, the night, and the wild, masculine beauty that stood in front of her. If she were under a spell, she had no desire to break it.

"There's no way that you're real," she murmured to his crotch.

He squatted down, much to her disappointment. With his face level to hers, she couldn't help but meet his eyes. "On the contrary, I'm very real," he replied, his eyes hot, heated, and filled with desire. She stared at him, puzzled.

Amanda forced her eyes away, staring at the tree in front of her. She'd once read an article that recommended staring at one to relieve stress. It wasn't working too well for her. Her heart was beating so fast she marveled at how it remained inside of her chest. "Why are you naked, then? Most people don't walk around the woods naked in the middle of the night."

He laughed, the sound rich and husky in the quiet of the night. His black hair was unfettered, brushing the tops of his muscular shoulders. It was so sexy she wanted to reach out and touch it... among other things. "Well, that explains it. I never could fit in with most people, not that I'd want to. Mainstream society is much too stifling for me."

Amanda glared at him, her breath hitching.

Damn, the man is gorgeous. It would be a shame to cover up a body like that. If he was comfortable with it, why not? Deciding to enjoy it while it lasted, she changed the subject. "I never did get the chance to thank you for rescuing me the other night. By the time the crowd had settled down, you were gone. I haven't seen you since then, so I thought maybe you were just passing through. Since you're here, though, I want to say thank you." Her voice trailed off as she blushed. She was rambling, and they both knew it.

He waved it away, but she could see her appreciation pleased him. "It's nothing another man wouldn't have done," he replied, his voice deep. Seductive. "If he had any balls to him."

Amanda blushed again. She didn't know about the rest, but this man certainly met that requirement. His were huge and hairless. He either shaved or waxed, and it was seriously sexy.

"I was out for a walk, and I decided to take a dip in the lake," he explained, breaking the silence. He looked away, giving Amanda the chance to admire the strong lines of his face. "I seem to have forgotten the exact spot I left my clothing." He stopped to shrug, a mischievous expression on his face. "I never expected to be discovered."

He shot a rueful glance at the area between his legs before meeting her eyes. Heat shot through her, nearly stifling her in the process. "Now that you've seen me naked, maybe it's time for us to introduce ourselves? My name is Ryker Connell. And you are?"

"Amanda Wyatt," she supplied, lowering her face to rub at her forehead. Ryker was a dream come true, but she was exhausted. Why couldn't something like this have happened before her illness? It was too little, too late, and she didn't have anything to offer a man, especially one as attractive as Ryker.

"Well, it was nice meeting you," she said politely, grasping the handle of her window as she prepared to roll it up. She dreaded the moment he left just as much as she hoped he would leave. The prospect of sleeping in her car was a horrible one, but she was exhausted enough to do it. Her body was too weary to stay awake much longer. "Maybe I'll see you around sometime."

"Wait," he said, his hand resting over the glass. "Why are you out here so late?" He leaned forward, slowly perusing the contents of her car.

His question brought it all back. She resented Jimmy, and the situation he'd placed her in. While she was out in the woods, he was dick deep in another female, enjoying the comforts of a place she'd helped to pay for. She closed her eyes in weariness. "I enjoy the quiet," she said, unwilling to share her problems with a stranger. "So I come out here when I want to be alone."

"Do you always bring your belongings?" His eyes flashed in the darkness, pinning her in place as he waited for her answer. *He knows*.

"How is that any of your business?" Amanda asked briskly, her fingers clenching the steering wheel.

In his eyes, she'd also seen pity and that bothered her more than anything. "Look, I'm not trying to be rude. I just don't like having to explain myself, especially to a total stranger."

"And I don't like leaving defenseless women out in the woods with nobody to protect them." His voice was firm as if he had reached some kind of decision. "I don't live too far from here, and if I had to guess I'd say you need some place to stay. I've got a spare room that I never use. It's yours for the night, no questions asked."

It was tempting. Although it was late, the night was sweltering hot. Mosquitoes were ambushing her left and right, by morning she'd be covered in bites. But how could she go home with a stranger? Indecisively, she stared at him as she attempted to weigh the pros and cons.

"What do you get out this?" her voice trembled as she spoke, but if she were honest it wasn't from fear. Ryker was the total package, she doubted there was a woman alive who could be within touching distance of his nude form and still keep her composure. Amanda forced her eyes to stay on his face, although she was tempted to let them drop. *God, I can only imagine the pleasures a woman has in his bed.* She blushed miserably, unaccustomed to thinking along those lines.

"I get the satisfaction of knowing I didn't leave someone to sleep out here," he shot back, coming to his feet. He stood up, but not before she'd seen the flash of victory in his eyes. He'd won this round, and he well knew it. But then again, it was likely he'd never doubted it. He was confident, a man used to having his own way.

He leaned over to give her directions to his house. Her eyes widened when she realized he was her neighbor. *Well, ex-neighbor. How ironic was that?* "I know where it is," she said, her voice hoarse. *Aroused.* She cleared her throat, embarrassed by the sensual tone. She sounded like a woman that had just been bedded... thoroughly.

The thought never crossed her mind that his offer contained anything more than a simple kindness. Why would it? A man like him could have any woman he desired, and he likely did. There was a raw, erotic air about him that made her believe he indulged often. He certainly wouldn't look twice at someone like her. *But why was he turned on?* She brushed the thought away. Maybe he had a high sex drive. It was likely he spent a great deal of time in that condition. He all but oozed sex and arousal.

He made no move to get in her car. Swallowing hard, she asked, "Are you going to ride with me?"

Ryker stared at the car with an expression of distaste. She knew her car was no great beauty, but damn. He looked as if he preferred torture to riding in it. "No," he informed her, shaking his head emphatically. "I know a shortcut to my place. I'll likely beat you back."

It must be one hell of a shortcut. They were miles away. Despite his confidence, she wondered how long she'd have to wait for him. "All right, thank you for the offer. I accept, but only for tonight. I'm in the middle of moving, but my new place isn't quite ready yet." That was the understatement of the year, but she couldn't think of anything else to say. Certainly, she had too much pride to ever admit to being thrown out.

Ryker watched her, a curious smile playing about his lips. It rattled her nerves. *Does he miss nothing?* She felt as if he'd seen right through her explanation. He saw too much, and it made her anxious. She was used to standing on her own two feet, and the thought of becoming a burden to anyone made her cringe. *But I won't be one to him.* The following day she'd have to find someplace else, no matter what.

"Didn't your mother ever tell you not to talk to strangers?" Amanda asked crossly, starting the car. She was uncomfortable and out of sorts with everything in her life, and completely unused to all the changes. Plus, she was exhausted.

Ryker laughed, his teeth bright and white in the darkness. "No," he replied, his voice deep and sincere. "It's more like she warned strangers not to talk to me." He turned and walked away as Amanda gaped at his rear. His cheeks were taut and smooth, and they begged for a woman's hands to grip them. She inhaled shakily. Her composure was shot.

"I'll see you back at the house," he called over his shoulder. Their eyes met as he winked before disappearing in the trees.

Chapter 5

Amanda pulled up in Ryker's driveway, parking close to the house. Turning the headlights and ignition off, she glanced around nervously. He wasn't there. Despite her initial doubt, she'd halfway expected him to be. His confidence was catching; he had a way of making a person believe he could do anything. "Get a grip, Amanda," she muttered to herself. "Next you'll be thinking the man can walk on water or something."

After a moment of debate, she finally decided to wait in the car for him. He hadn't given her any reason to distrust him, but she didn't know him that well. Ryker was different, something more than other men she'd seen, she just hoped that was a good thing. Putting her trust into someone that she'd just met was difficult. Amanda cast a wary look at the house but she couldn't see any irate person brandishing a gun. She relaxed just a fraction of an inch. So far, so good. It would appear it really was his house.

And what a house it was. She'd always admired it on her drives, but who wouldn't? Made of brick, the house had an expansive yard with a cobblestone walkway. It was beautiful enough to appease a female, but with the barn, shed, and garage it was rugged enough to appeal to a man. Standing two stories high it was huge, nearly too much for a man living on his own. Was Ryker married? The thought disturbed her.

The front door opened to reveal his tall form. He'd dressed, although casually. He wore a plain white t-shirt and athletic shorts, but his feet were bare when he stepped out. The material from his shirt stretched across his wide shoulders and muscular arms, while his shorts displayed his lean hips and thighs to perfection. Ryker was solid, his body in the best physical condition possible, and it showed. She admired the view for another moment before stepping out of the car.

    She smiled shyly as he stopped in front of her, her eyes flickering away from his face to look toward the house. "You have a lovely home," she said, telling him the first thing that popped to her mind.

    "I like it," he replied, shrugging his shoulders. He turned toward her trunk with an eyebrow raised in inquiry. "If you'll tell me what you'd like to bring in, I can take it in for you."

    "Okay," Amanda replied, feeling gauche. She handed over her keys before running her sweaty hands down her jeans. "Just that overnight bag there," she said, pointing at mid-sized backpack covered in a floral pattern. It was lucky that she'd kept it packed up, otherwise she would have needed to dig through everything. "It won't hurt to leave the rest out here since I'll only be here for such a short time." She kept her medicines in her purse.

    He didn't reply as he opened the trunk to grab it. He held out her keys as he gestured toward the front door, waiting until she moved before falling into step next to her. "Are you from Nashoba?" Ryker's voice was curious, as if he'd been giving it some thought.

"Not originally," she admitted. "I'm from the East Coast, but I decided to leave my hometown after my parents died. There was really nothing to hold me there, not even a house. My parents didn't own our home, they just rented it. Once everything was settled, I packed up what was mine and left. I planned on going to California. Along the way I happened to stop in Nashoba for fuel, and I ended up meeting Jean. She was looking for a bartender, and I took a chance and stayed. That was a little over six years ago. What about you?"

"I'm from Germany, believe it or not." That explained his sexy accent. That man had a decadent voice, so seductively lethal that she thought about sex every time he spoke.

She stepped inside with Ryker following, a gasp escaping her lips at her first sight of the pleasant surroundings. Everything looked new, the interior designed to be warm and inviting. He smiled at her gasp, but otherwise he remained silent. After a moment, he walked into the living room, placing her bag on the couch.

Amanda followed him, her eyes trying to take it all in at once. "Wow," she muttered appreciatively. "If I had a house like this, I'm not sure I'd ever want to leave my home." She spun around to face him. "Do you live here by yourself?" Realizing it might be too personal, she added, "Sorry, I'm not trying to pry."

He waved it off with one large hand. "I don't mind your question. I live here alone, but I haven't been here long. I just purchased the place a few months ago."

"Oh," Amanda replied. "But how long have you lived in Nashoba? I don't remember seeing you before that night in the bar." And she would have remembered someone like him. He was the type of man that would always draw attention, not only because of his good looks but because of his confidence.

"Oh, I'm definitely not a newcomer," he grinned. "I've lived in this area for years. Before I bought this place, I lived about fifteen minutes outside of town."

"You're not Amish, are you?" Amanda immediately felt foolish. Of course he wasn't. An Amish man would have never been in a bar or swimming in a lake in the middle of the night.

His grin turned into a chuckle. "Definitely not that," he mock-cringed, rubbing at the shadow of beard growth on his firm chin. "I'm way too uninhibited for that kind of life."

He motioned toward the couch, his expression turning serious. "Why don't you take a seat? I'll go get some refreshments." His eyes slid slowly across her, from the top of her head and down to her feet before settling back on her face. Funny, he acted as if he enjoyed staring at her. She wasn't used to that kind of attention.

Amanda was hungry and weary, but the weariness won. She picked up her bag from the couch, turning back to face him. "I appreciate the offer, but to tell you the truth I am exhausted. Would you mind very much if I just went to bed? As late as it is, you must be tired, too."

He nodded slowly, his eyes thoughtful. An eerie feeling washed over her at his appraisal. In his eyes she felt exposed, as if he knew all. What would this gorgeous, kind man say if he knew the real truth about her? Even more, what would it feel like to actually have someone she could confide in, without fear of distaste or revulsion? She couldn't bring herself to do it, though. Emotionally, she wasn't sure she could handle it. She'd already been through too much. She couldn't stand for him to see her as anything less than a healthy female.

* * * * *

After showing Amanda to her room, Ryker reluctantly left her behind. Walking down the carpeted hallway he stopped to enter his own room, his thoughts consumed with his guest. He couldn't get her out of his mind.

He was stunned by his offer. Ryker wasn't used to having overnight guests. In fact, he wasn't used to having guests at all, although his home was certainly large enough to accommodate them. He valued his solitude, especially after a long shift with some of the more mischievous guardians. Especially the younger ones. Even in their fifties, many of them still acted like children. His head ached from thinking about their outlandish pranks and jokes.

Amanda's presence didn't disturb him. If anything it relieved him. She was vulnerable, he could see it in her eyes. Something troubled her, and it was much worse than the breakup she'd just experienced. Ryker couldn't quite put his finger on it, but all was not well with the female. He was just glad she'd agreed to come back with him willingly. He wouldn't have been able to leave her. It went against the grain for him, not only as a wolf but as a man. Had she turned him down, he would have been forced to get more creative.

But she is leaving tomorrow, Ryker reminded himself. It wasn't as if their arrangement was permanent. For some reason, the thought bothered him. Greatly.

* * * * *

The next morning Amanda walked down the stairs quietly, her overnight bag slung over her shoulder. Despite the events of the night, she'd slept like the dead, but who wouldn't have? The bed was huge, the mattress comfortable. It wouldn't be a hardship for anyone to live in a quiet, comfortable home like his, but she didn't let herself consider it. Everything about his world was foreign. She simply didn't belong.

Her cheek was sore, but it could have been a lot worse. She'd made her face up carefully to conceal the light purple bruise across her cheek. It wouldn't be visible inside the bar, and that's all that mattered. It wasn't likely she'd see anyone until evening anyhow.

Leaving the last step behind, she crept toward the front door. It was better to leave now, while Ryker was still asleep. The man knew too much already, his blue eyes saw too much for her to ever be comfortable in his presence. If she didn't leave him now, he'd have questions——questions she wasn't willing to answer.

Where will I go? Amanda didn't know. She'd been paid the day before, but it automatically went into the checking account she shared with Jimmy. The account was empty, she already knew that. Jimmy had texted her the day before to tell her, but he hadn't told her where the money had gone to.

I have nobody to blame but myself. How could she have been so blind? Young and inexperienced, she'd practically agreed to anything he asked of her, even if it hurt her in the process. She'd done all that and more for a man who didn't care less about her. The night before had convinced her of that.

With the exception of being homeless, Amanda really wasn't as upset about their relationship ending as she'd always thought she'd be. *Since when?* She didn't know, but somewhere down the line she'd fallen out of love with him. In many ways, their break up was a relief. No longer did she have to live her life constantly trying to please a man that could never be satisfied. Let him screw every woman in Nashoba, if he wanted to. Jimmy was no longer her problem.

Reaching out to twist the doorknob, Amanda was startled when Ryker asked blandly, "Going somewhere?"

With a gasp she spun around, her pulse racing. "I didn't know you were awake," she told him, her fingers clenching the straps of her overnight bag to keep it from sliding off of her shoulder. "Yes, I was leaving. Thank you again for your hospitality, but I don't want to overstay my welcome."

He watched her closely, reminding Amanda of a cat stalking a mouse. Then he smiled as if he found her reaction amusing. It did wonderful things to his already attractive face. "Nonsense," he said, beckoning for her to follow him. "I can't let you leave without eating. What kind of host would I be?"

Amanda turned to look back at the door once more before following him into his sparkling clean kitchen. "What would you like? I have fruits, cereal, or I could cook you something," he added, somewhat reluctantly. "Of course I can't guarantee you'll survive it."

The last part was said so seriously that Amanda froze. He chuckled, breaking the mood. "I do make a mean steak, though."

"I'll just have some fruit and a glass of water, please," she told him, sliding onto a kitchen stool. She leaned over to drop her bag on the floor before straightening back up to watch him. He was wearing a tight pair of stonewashed jeans and another t-shirt. Ryker was sexy as hell. He was hot but nice, a combination that was virtually unheard of.

He slid a glass bowl of assorted fruits in her direction before placing a glass of water right in front of her. "Feel free to eat as many as you would like. *Please.* I'm not much of a fruit eater."

"Then why did you buy them?" she asked curiously, taking a banana.

Ryker shrugged. "Doesn't everybody?"

He had a point there. Growing up, Amanda remembered her mom always buying fruit, but they never did eat it all. A lot was thrown out, but it didn't stop her mother from buying more. People were creatures of habit. They thought they should buy it, so they did, even if they didn't necessarily want it.

With a cup of coffee in his hand, he sat down across from her, his intense blue eyes immediately settling on her face. "So, tell me about this new place of yours." It was a demand not a question.

Amanda choked on her fruit, her eyes immediately watering as she attempted to cough it up. Furiously, she coughed, her face turning red from exertion and embarrassment. After several seconds she choked it up. Ryker watched it all.

Grabbing the glass of water, she took a long sip from it as she thought about his question. Amanda hated being put on the spot, especially considering she had no place to go. "Why?" she asked, her voice raspy.

"Why not?" he countered smoothly, sipping at his coffee.

She laid her fruit down, her appetite gone. His question reminded her of how hopeless her current situation was. "Thanks for breakfast," she told him, leaning over to grab her bag.

"Not yet," he said, shaking his head. His hair was so black that it almost appeared blue in the bright sunlight from the windows. "Look, I think we just need to talk straight, wouldn't you agree?"

He continued without giving her a chance to reply. "When I discovered you last night, you were out in the middle of nowhere with a car full of your belongings. If that wasn't telling enough, the left side of your face would have cleared up any confusion," his voice deepened on the last part as if the thought of her being struck made him angry.

Leaning forward, he locked her in place with his piercing eyes. "My gut instinct is telling me that you don't have any place to go. Am I correct?"

Amanda swallowed hard, immediately forgetting about leaving. She was tired, not physically tired so much as mentally, and her problems seemed overwhelming. Why couldn't she share them with this complete stranger? She was tired of carrying the load, she needed to unburden herself. She wouldn't tell him everything, but she could tell him some.

"My boyfriend broke up with me last night," she told him quietly, her fingers wrapped around the glass in front of her. "We lived together. He wanted me out."

Confessing that she'd been dumped was worse than she'd imagined. Jimmy hadn't considered her good enough, and now the whole world would know it. Amanda tilted her chin up, refusing to let Ryker know how much it bothered her.

"I see," he replied in a neutral tone of voice, slowly taking another sip from his cup. Amanda had never been a coffee drinker, but combined with his masculine scent, she would never look at it the same again. Ryker smelled good, his woodsy scent pleasing. She fought the urge to just close her eyes and inhale deeply.

His firm lips tightened into a grimace, his eyes narrowing in on the left side of her face. "Did he give you that bruise, too?"

Her hand flew up to her face, cupping her cheek gently. "You can still see it?" she asked him in horror. If he could see it so would Jean, and that would lead to a whole lot of questions she didn't want to answer.

"I saw it last night," he replied. "You've done a great job of covering it up today, though." His eyes slid slowly over her face, the heat from his gaze affecting her oddly. Her very blood was turning to molten lava. She felt languid, even sensual, and the man hadn't even touched her. *I'm losing it*, she thought to herself. What on earth was wrong with her? She was lusting after a stranger, and not even one she had a chance in hell of having.

"You're not considering going back to him, are you?" His entire body seemed to stiffen, right in front of Amanda's eyes.

"God, no," she replied, shaking her head in bemusement. The thought had never crossed her mind. "Besides, he's living with somebody else now."

"His loss."

Amanda knew that Jimmy wouldn't have seen it that way, but she didn't bother to correct him.

"Is that why you wear long-sleeves and turtlenecks?" His eyes slid across her chest and stomach, as if he could see the skin underneath. Her nipples pebbled underneath the material of the shirt, the weight of her breasts suddenly heavy. The room felt hot, and it was only getting hotter by the second. *Can he see the reaction I'm having to him*? Even more, what would he do about it? Finding the possibilities too interesting to contemplate, she slammed the lid on her thoughts as she casually crossed her arms on the counter in front of her chest.

"Are you ill?" he asked her, his tone gruff with concern. Amanda started to shake her head, but then reconsidered. Just like Jean, he'd just given her the perfect excuse. "I wear turtlenecks because I like them, it doesn't matter what season it is. And now that you've mentioned it, I have been feeling a bit under the weather. It's just a summer cold, nothing more."

Her eyes lifted to his. "Last night was the first time Jimmy ever laid a hand on me," she told him truthfully, careful to keep the tremor of hurt out of her voice. Discussing her problems with Jimmy could end up deadly for the other man. Ryker was already upset, telling him more would just be adding fuel to the fire. "Just because I'm not hot or anything doesn't mean that I would put up with someone abusing me. Contrary to popular belief, being overweight doesn't mean desperate."

He lifted his dark eyebrow up at her as he took another sip of his coffee. His lips slid around the smooth edge, forming the perfect seal. He'd shaved sometime since she'd last seen him, and it only accentuated the perfection of his features. Amanda shifted uncomfortably on her seat, almost gasping out loud as the seam of her jeans brushed against her swollen clit. *Could any man have a more sensual mouth than his?* She doubted it. She'd certainly never seen one, and she'd watched quite a few men passing through the doors of the bar.

"Well, there's only one solution to this problem," he told her, placing his coffee cup down with a firm thump. "You'll have to stay here."

* * * * *

Amanda gaped back at him, her large eyes shocked. Ryker ignored her reaction in favor of admiring their color. Her eyes were a lighter blue than his, reminding him of clear skies on a sunny day. *It would be easy for a man to get lost in their depths.* Heavy-lidded, Amanda naturally had bedroom eyes, and his thoughts seemed to center around dragging her to the nearest one to have his wicked way with her curvaceous body.

He wasn't a virgin, not by a long shot, but he was acting like one. He couldn't stop fantasizing about finding his way between her full legs. *When was the last time I was so stimulated by a female?* He couldn't recall. Women and sex came to him easily; he'd spent his entire adult life enjoying sensual pleasures. As a werewolf that meant lifetimes... he'd been in more beds than he could ever count.

Ryker was treading a thin line by keeping a temptation like her so close, but he powerless to stop it. Although she wasn't his mate, he was compellingly attracted to her. So much so he couldn't even stand up from his seat. His hardened shaft pulsated painfully against the constricting material of his jeans. At this rate, his zipper would be permanently imprinted on his shaft. *Unless I seduce her.*

Just thinking about it made him ache in ways he'd never ached before. He imagined ripping her turtleneck straight down the middle, exposing the full breasts underneath. Her breasts were the perfect size, they'd be more than big enough to fill his hands while he suckled her tight nipples. Ryker nearly groaned out loud at the thought.

"Hello?" Amanda said, waving her hand up and down to gain his attention. "Are you listening? I can't stay here with you."

"Why not?" Ryker asked her, pleased that his voice didn't give him away.

She quieted at his question as if she were searching for any excuse to grasp onto. "It just wouldn't be right," she finally replied. "You've been kind to let me stay here for the night, but I can't take advantage of that."

"Actually, you wouldn't be," he replied calmly, using the first excuse he could come up with. "I work quite a bit, and I don't like leaving my home unattended. You'd actually be doing me a favor."

She watched him warily as she waited for him to continue. "I'll be going out-of-town at some point in the next several weeks, and I need someone to be here while I'm gone. You're actually the perfect solution to my problem. If you'll agree to stay, it will save me a great deal of time."

"But you don't know me," she told him in a low voice, her fingers clenching the glass in front of her. "If I were you I wouldn't entrust a place like this to anyone, especially someone I'd just met."

Ryker almost smiled at her words, but he was careful to conceal it. *If only she knew.* The wolf that lived within him was able to sense a great deal about her, and what he couldn't the man could. She was a truthful woman, a woman with a great deal of pride and self-respect. She was also wary enough of people in general to keep her personal life secret. She'd watch over and protect his home like a female wolf would her den. Of that, he had no doubt.

He'd been concerned about her scent and her health, but she'd reassured him. Any illness altered a human's natural smell, although it was light enough that the average person wasn't aware of it. He wasn't human, though, and he could scent things that they couldn't. There was a lot he knew about Amanda already, much more than she'd ever realize.

"I'm an excellent judge of character," he told her smoothly. "And I have no concerns over you assuming the role of caretaker. Naturally, your room and board will be included. You'll have a weekly budget set aside to take care of any necessities, including any groceries that you might need. I don't expect you to cook or clean, though. I have a cook and two maids that take care of all of that."

He gestured toward the fruit bowl ruefully before adding, "You can see that I'm not much of a shopper, but I've recently asked the cook to take over the task. If you prefer to do this, just let me know. Or you can give her a list of what you need, and she can take care of it. Whichever way works best for you."

A wide range of emotions flitted across her face as she considered his words. Ryker saw surprise, hope, and then relief. Her income was likely limited. After all, how much could a bartender in a small town like Nashoba really make? Certainly not enough to maintain a comfortable lifestyle. He could give that to her, if she were willing to accept it.

And his words had held some truth to them. Sometime soon he'd accompany Alexander to the challenge, and there was every possibility that he'd have to fight, too. If Alexander failed, it would all fall on Ryker's shoulders. He'd have to beat his opponent, and it wouldn't be easy. Challenges usually meant a fight to the death. There was no guarantee that either one of them would return.

"Where do you work?" she asked him suddenly, much to his surprise.

"I'm in forestry. I work outside of Nashoba,

about fifteen minutes out." Ryker didn't elaborate any further.

"You don't hear that every day. I didn't know you guys worked out there, but it makes sense. This place is nothing but forests and trees."

If you only knew what goes on in these woods, especially during the full moon. "So will you accept my offer?" Ryker held his breath as he awaited her response.

Amanda exhaled heavily. She didn't immediately respond, and for a moment, he wondered if she would refuse his offer. He hoped not. He was determined to have her, whether she realized it or not.

"I agree," she told him, her voice somber. "But I can't commit to forever. I'll stay for the next month or two, but no longer than that."

"Sounds good to me," he replied, unable to conceal his satisfaction. "If you'll get me your keys, I'll bring the rest of your stuff in."

Chapter 6

Alexander placed the phone back on the charger in the silent meeting room, his expression resigned. He exchanged a long look with Ryker before facing the other pack members that sat around the table. Each one of them stared back at Alexander with puzzled expressions on their faces but not Ryker. He was already aware of the king's troubles. The entire pack would know, too, before the night was over.

Alexander's wife and mate, Carole Anne, sat by his side, her belly slightly swollen with their first child. Originally human, she'd been brought into the pack after Alexander discovered her living in a cabin not too far away from Wolf Town. Fate had blessed him. Carole Anne had adapted well to life as a werewolf, and she was well-liked by the wolves.

"I know you are wondering why I called you here," Alexander said grimly, clasping his hands together loosely in front of him. "And I'm about to appease your curiosity. As you probably heard just now, we're having problems with the Australian pack. Unfortunately, these problems have escalated, and it now requires drastic action to resolve."

"What do you mean, Alexander?" Ivan asked, a frown marring his smooth forehead. Looking at the two men together, it would be easy to believe they were twins. They weren't. Despite his youthful appearance, Ivan was Alexander's grandfather, and the former King of Wolf Town. Ivan now spent his time in the background, content to give Alexander advice when the younger wolf requested it.

"To sum it up, I've been challenged by the Australian pack for my role as king," he replied unhappily, ignoring the gasps that filled the room. "They seem to think I've failed the wolves as a whole, and they believe they could do better. They've already selected my opponent. Some of you might know him. His name is Balor."

"This is bullshit!" Ivan roared, his fist hitting the table. The heavy wood shuddered, but it didn't break. The poor table had been through hell. They were lucky it was constructed for meetings between supernatural creatures as was most of the furniture at headquarters. Otherwise they would have been shit out of luck, with no furniture to use.

"What do you mean you've been challenged?" Ivan continued, his face contorting slightly in anger. "You've done an outstanding job at holding the packs together, especially through the trials and tribulations we've experienced this past year. No, I don't believe this has anything to do with your actions as king," Ivan said thoughtfully. "It's more likely that someone has aspirations for your title, and they will use anything or anyone in their quest to get it."

"I've wondered the same thing," Alexander admitted, his voice somber. "Especially given the circumstances their challenge is based off of. I've wracked my brain in an attempt to discover where I went wrong, and I'm just drawing blanks."

"You aren't in the wrong," Ivan said, standing up to pace back and forth. "But I don't believe that's the point. I'm willing to bet this challenge was issued out of greed and nothing more. You couldn't have done anything to avoid it. They were determined to make a play, and they have. Now, we just need to focus on making sure the right king remains on the throne."

"What is a challenge, Alexander?" Carole Anne spoke up, a hand resting on her swollen stomach. Her face was pale as she stared at her husband. "And why haven't you told me about this before?"

Alexander closed his eyes and exhaled deeply. He looked tormented, as if he dreaded explaining more than anything. Ryker sympathized with the other male. He couldn't imagine what it had to be like, telling your pregnant mate that there was a chance you wouldn't be alive to watch the birth of your first child. Alexander was in a hellish predicament.

"The Australian pack wants to replace me as king," he said softly, gently taking her hand as he watched her. "And I'm not going to mince words, Carole Anne. I'll have to fight my competitor, and it will be a fight to the death. Only one of us will walk away, but I'm going to do everything in my power to make sure it's me."

"Oh, God, no," she exclaimed, her free hand moving up to press against her lips. She stared at Alexander in horror, but Ryker had to give her credit. She didn't beg him to stay, which said a lot for Carole Anne. Instead, she came to her feet and hurried to the door as she muttered, "Excuse me." The door shut quietly behind her as she left the room.

Alexander stood up to pursue her, but Ivan stopped him with a hand on his arm. "Let her go, son," he told him, casting a concerned look at the door. "She needs time to process this, and she wants to do it alone. Carole Anne will be okay. She'll let you know if she's not."

After a moment, Alexander nodded. He sat back down in his seat, his expression composed. Ryker had to admire his self-control. He wasn't sure he could have done the same, had he found himself in the other man's position.

"I'll give her a little while," Alexander finally said. "But if she's not back soon, I'm going after her. Even if she weren't pregnant, something like this would be a tremendous shock. The stress isn't good for my mate or my child."

They all nodded, each one understanding the risks. Female werewolves didn't get pregnant easily; it wasn't uncommon for it to take a hundred years to conceive. The entire pack was still reeling over how quickly the queen had gotten pregnant. Some speculated it was because she was originally human, but who really knew?

"My liege, have you already selected your second?" Marrok asked as all eyes turned toward him. He was known as a quiet and reserved werewolf. Ryker liked him immensely. "If not, I'd be happy to volunteer for the position."

"Thank you, Marrok, for your offer. But even if I hadn't already selected someone, I wouldn't take you up on it." Alexander sent a pointed look around the table. "Choosing a second is not an easy process. We all know it's dangerous, possibly deadly, which is why I am determined to select someone without a mate."

"Who did you pick?" Connor asked, his eyes moving from person to person. When they reached Ryker, they widened. *He knows.*

"I've asked Ryker to be my second," Alexander informed them, leaning back in his chair to peruse them all. "And he agreed. He's unmated, but I didn't ask him because he's any less important to the pack. Just because he doesn't have his mate now doesn't mean he never will. Somewhere out there, she's waiting. I'd hate for her to lose her true mate just because he died defending my right to be king."

His words gave Ryker pause. He'd never considered it that way before, but it didn't make any difference in his decision. He was just a little over five hundred years old, but he'd yet to meet his mate. And with each century that passed him by, his hopes of ever finding her dwindled. *Some werewolves are just meant to be single.* At least it seemed that way to him.

Amanda's face swam in front of him, her delectable curves replaying in his mind. Nearly two weeks had passed since he'd invited her to stay, and he hadn't regretted his decision. But then again, he'd hardly seen her. His guardian duties had increased dramatically due to the upcoming challenge, and he hadn't realized just how much she worked. It's wasn't uncommon for the human female to work twelve hour shifts, or sometimes even more. She was often gone before he ever got home, and she didn't return until the early morning hours. *No wonder she always looks exhausted.*

It didn't seem fair that she devoted so much of her life to the bar in exchange for the pitifully small wages she earned in return. Especially considering the painfully short life span of the average human. It was a plight he'd seen time and time again.

No matter how someone looked at it, poverty was a horrible way to live. It didn't matter if it was the sixteenth-century or the twenty-first, poverty didn't care about things like time. It destroyed entire lives. There was nothing worse than worrying about where your next meal would be coming from or living with the constant fear of losing your home.

If anyone could understand, Ryker could. The centuries hadn't dulled the pain of losing his parents early in life, just because of poverty. Ryker had been fifteen when they'd died. The teenage years were particularly hard on a werewolf, and he hadn't had anyone to guide him through it. Ryker had been forced to survive the best way he could.

The early sixteenth-century had been a dangerous time for werewolves. In those days, anyone viewed as different was heavily persecuted by superstitious peasants. Ryker cringed at the thought of how many innocents had died, both human and werewolf alike.

His pack had been forced to disband when Ryker was just a child. He'd spent his childhood watching his mother and father work themselves into exhaustion to keep a roof over their heads, all the while always looking over their shoulders in fear that their secret would be discovered. And the full moons had been the worst. Forced by the wolf that lived within them to shift, it had one day turned deadly.

Spotted by a wandering peasant, he'd been quick to alert the village to the monsters that lived within their midst. They immediately took action. The villagers went from door to door demanding entry just to search their homes. It hadn't taken them long to force their way into Ryker's home.

His parents had sacrificed themselves for him. Aware of the danger that surrounded their only child, they'd distracted the villagers by making an appearance, leading them away just enough for Ryker to escape. And then they'd let themselves be taken, knowing it was the only way to give him enough time to get away.

The pain that washed over him was as fresh as it had been that first few years. If they hadn't been poor, they could have left Germany altogether. But despite their best efforts, there never was enough. And in their poverty they had found their deaths, leaving him behind to face an uncertain future.

Grief-stricken, Ryker had wandered aimlessly, taking on any position he could just to keep his belly full. And in those days he'd discovered just how depraved humanity could be. As a young man he'd been vulnerable, both physically and mentally, and he had to protect himself against those that would have used him in an ill manner. The streets were no place for children of any age, even back then.

But he'd survived, and he had amassed a fortune in the process. Never would his children be caught in the hopelessness and despair of poverty, he'd made sure of that. But would he ever get the chance to have any?

"When can we expect this event to take place?" Connor asked, yanking Ryker from his thoughts. He shifted uncomfortably in his chair, but none of the others seemed to notice his temporary lack of attention. Their attention was focused on Alexander, with varying looks of dismay on their faces.

"The date hasn't been set," Alexander replied. "But that's not uncommon. If I had to guess, I would say sometime in the next month or two. Right now, the Australian pack is notifying every pack in the world of their intent to challenge me. Most of them will want to send someone to represent their pack at the challenge... and to pledge their loyalties to the winner. These things take time, everything has to go through the proper channels. If the Australian pack issued a challenge without notifying the other packs, there would be every possibility that they wouldn't acknowledge the validity of it. That's the last thing they would want."

"I think I speak for all of us when I say that we'd like to accompany you," Connor said, looking around the room for confirmation. All of the men nodded, some of them even snarling at the thought of going.

"I wouldn't have it any other way." Alexander looked pleased at their support. "If your women will let you go," he added as an afterthought, with a grin.

The mated males groaned. "I would rather participate in the challenge," Marrok told the others, his deep voice solemn. "It would be a lot easier than telling Taylor she has to stay behind."

Connor scoffed. "Man, you are really whipped," he told Marrok, his face disgusted. "Grow some balls and lay down the law. You're acting like a big baby."

The room grew quiet. Even Alexander watched the two men in a mixture of awe and amusement. Their bickering and arguments were notorious amongst the guardians. Generally, Connor was the one to start them... But Marrok almost always finished it.

Marrok swung his face toward Connor, his black eyes cold and deadly. He was considered to be one of the scariest guardians they had, and with good reason. A man could see his own death in those dark depths and once they did, any battle was as good as over.

It didn't stop Connor, though. Then again he was probably immune to it, after having spent years pissing off Marrok on a near-daily basis.

Marrok's lip curled up in repugnance an instant before he said, "Really, Connor, *really*? You think you have any room to talk? Excuse me, but aren't you the man that has to run into the bathroom daily, just to hang his face over the toilet because he has morning sickness? And what about the stockpile of cherry and chocolate ice cream in the office freezer, you know, the ones that you've been pigging out on? Because of your *food cravings*." Marrok made a quote sign with his fingers, much to everyone's amusement.

The other guardians laughed, even Alexander. "And here I thought Natalie carried the baby," Orlando said loudly, in a mock whisper. "Imagining Connor pregnant is not a pretty thought. Especially when it comes to the delivery part."

Connor growled, but Alexander cut him off with a stern look in his direction. "That's enough, children. Advise your females of the situation," he told the room in general. "We'll be increasing our training sessions over the next several weeks. I want to make sure that all of us are in top condition," he stressed the last part, with a pointed look at Connor's midsection.

* * * * *

Amanda closed the front door behind her, sagging against it on trembling legs. She'd gone to her chemotherapy treatment as usual, but she'd received bad news. The cancer wasn't responding as anticipated. Her doctor had wanted to add on radiation, and she had agreed. She hadn't expected the side effects to be so bad, though.

It had taken everything she had just to make the drive back to Ryker's home. Amanda couldn't recall ever feeling sicker. The stairs across from her wavered in the late afternoon sunlight, and she questioned her ability to even make it up them.

Her purse slid from her shoulder and fell in the floor, but Amanda didn't try to pick it up. Using her last reserves of strength, she walked unsteadily toward the stairs. Nausea churned inside of her, some of it bubbling up enough to reach the back of her throat. Attempting to hold it back, she grasped the rail and prayed she wouldn't vomit. As weak as she was, she wouldn't be able to clean it up. *What would Ryker think of me then?*

Thinking about him seemed to strengthen her. Moving slowly, she took the stairs one at a time. Little did he know, but his offer to let her stay had actually been a blessing. After having spent nearly two weeks there, she could say it with a certainty. And despite her cancer, she was happy. Here in his home, she felt a peace she hadn't experienced in years. The last thing she wanted to do was ruin it.

Ryker hadn't been exaggerating when he said he worked a lot. She'd rarely seen him, and even then it had only been in passing. The thought left her deflated. Ryker was attractive, and she was attracted. It was foolish, there was no possibility that anything besides their arrangement could exist between the two of them. Still, though, there was that small little voice that wished the impossible wasn't quite so impossible.

Although she felt disappointed by his continued absence, she also felt relieved. It was clear that she was nursing some type of crazy crush. Spending any real amount of time with Ryker would only increase her attraction to him, and eventually he'd pick up on it, embarrassing them both. Who knew? Maybe he'd already sensed it and was purposely avoiding her. It really was for the best. If she weren't careful she'd end up ruining her living arrangements and that would be a disaster.

Cresting the top step, Amanda swayed dizzily as she fought to catch her breath. Fearing she'd fall back the way she came, she forced herself down the hallway, her eyes locked on her door. The doctor had warned her that the combination of chemo and radiation would be harsher on her body, but she hadn't expected it to be that bad. And even worse, she'd been too sick to pick up her newest prescriptions.

Reaching her doorway, Amanda knew her luck was up. Shoving the door open, she ran for her private bathroom, but she was an instant too late. Dropping to her knees she emptied her stomach, breathing painfully in between the heaves.

She lowered her head onto her outstretched arm, tears rolling down her face. Nausea continued to churn within her exhausted body and her stomach burned. *Will it never end?* She was weary and exhausted, but she still had a mess to clean up.

The room spun around, much to her stomach's distress. She was too weak to get up off of the floor, much to her horror. Sliding to the side of the toilet she stretched out on her side, continuing to cradle her head on her arm. Surprisingly, the cool tiles felt good against her skin. It was her last waking thought. Too sick to stay awake, she met the darkness, blissfully relieved to have an escape from her awareness.

Chapter 7

Ryker darted across the sidewalk and up the steps, easily taking them two at a time. He was pumped up from the meeting, and anticipating Alexander's promises of additional practice times. The werewolves got pretty physical during training. He couldn't wait to kick some ass.

Of course his eagerness had nothing to do with Amanda's car parked in the driveway, or so he told himself. It had to be her night off... finally. As early in the evening as it was, there was no way she could possibly be in bed yet. He'd find her and play it by ear, but no matter what it took Ryker was determined to get to know his new roommate. And if he were really lucky, the night would end with the two of them extremely acquainted. Preferably in bed, but Ryker wasn't picky. The couch, kitchen table, or even the stairs would work just as well... especially with his skills.

Really, seducing his roommate was probably not his smartest idea, not that he had any experience with it. Before Amanda he'd never lived with any woman – except for his mother. Once he had her out of his system, though, their living arrangements could easily get sticky. He wasn't sure he'd even have attempted it, if it weren't for her determination to leave.

He stopped at the door, his hand on the knob. *Who am I trying to fool?* As badly as he desired her, he would have still attempted it. Nothing was going to satisfy his lust except fulfilling it.

Opening the door, he immediately came to a halt at the sight of her discarded purse on the floor. At the same time, his nostrils were assailed by the sickeningly sweet smell of poison. His every sense went on alert, his eyes scanning the rooms and doorways. The scent he associated with Amanda had strengthened to toxic levels, nearly eradicating her natural pheromones. *What in the hell is going on?* None of it made sense.

He scooped her purse off the floor before placing it on the corner table. Closing the door behind him, he followed her trail as he sped up the stairs. His steps were so quiet the average human wouldn't have even known he was there.

The house was completely quiet. His cook and maids would have left hours before, as efficient as they were it didn't take them long to maintain his home. He couldn't scent anyone else inside, lucky for them. It would have been a lethal mistake for anyone to invade his home uninvited.

Still, the tension didn't leave him. Ryker was wound up as tight as a spring, deep within he just knew that something was not right. He approached the open door to her room, and when he reached the doorway he frowned. There were no signs of life, but she was there. Her scent was too strong for her not to be.

The bathroom door was opened, although it

was quiet inside. Stalking across the room, he flipped on the light to reveal the unconscious woman on the floor.

"Amanda," he hissed urgently, moving quickly to lift her up. Her head fell back against his arm, revealing a pale face marred with deep purple circles underneath her eyes. He ignored the proof of her illness on the floor and toilet. The mess meant nothing to him, but it did increase his worry. *Was she truly poisoned?* It certainly appeared so.

He turned to carry her to her bed. She was deathly still. If not for her shallow breaths, he would have believed her to be dead. She didn't stir at all, not even when he placed her on top of the comforter.

It only took a second for Ryker to grab his phone and call headquarters. Marrok answered immediately, much to his relief. The other man would be professional and quick to act, unlike some of the younger guardians that often worked the evening shift.

"Marrok, it's Ryker," he said quickly, his eyes never leaving Amanda's face. "I need one of the doctors quickly. It's a life or death situation."

"One moment," Marrok responded, putting the line on hold. Ryker knew the protocol. The other man was transferring him directly to the doctor's station, but he would also put the facility on a code blue. That meant that everyone there would be prepared for anything that might go down, until the emergency was over.

The phone only rang once before it was

answered. "Doctor Sanders," the other man said, in a clipped voice. He got straight to the point. "What is your emergency?"

"Doctor Sanders, this is Ryker," he informed him, pressing two fingers to Amanda's neck. Her heartbeat was there, but it was distant. "I've got an emergency at my home. I need you to get your ass over here, ASAP."

"What's the problem?" In the background, he was gathering stuff together. When it came to Wolf Town's doctors, they could always be relied on to move fast. "And who is the wolf?"

"It's not a wolf," Ryker responded immediately. "It's a human female. From her scent, I believe she's been poisoned. I found her unconscious on the bathroom floor. At some point she vomited, but not since I've been here. She's unconscious, and I can't wake her up." Even to his own ears, his voice was filled with worry. He couldn't have cared less.

"I'll be there in fifteen minutes," Doctor Sanders bit out, an instant before the line disconnected. Ryker tossed the phone on the bedside table, feeling more helpless than he'd ever felt before. Would she even last the fifteen minutes it would take the other man to reach them? He didn't need to be a medical professional to realize he was losing her.

He ran back into the bathroom, wetting and wringing out several washcloths before rushing back to her. Gently he cleaned her face and her hands before deciding to change her. If nothing else, he could make her as comfortable as possible. He wished he could do more.

In the wardrobe, he found a long nightgown. It was made of a soft, stretchy type of material. It would work. Ryker turned back to face her, his hands trembling. In the span of five hundred years, he'd fought some of the fiercest battles possible, but none of them had unnerved him like her unresponsiveness did.

Unbuttoning her shirt, he lifted her upper half to pull it off. His eyes widened when he saw the port at the top of her chest. He leaned forward for a better look, but for the life of him he wasn't sure what it was for. He quickly dismissed it. It wasn't important, at least not at that time.

Her bra and jeans quickly joined her shirt. As efficiently as possible, he cleaned her face and arms before carefully easing the nightgown over her head. To his surprise, her hair shifted. Before he could free it from the confines of the material it fell, revealing the bald surface underneath.

His hands stilled, his eyes locked on her skull as he stood frozen in shock. After a second, his lips tightened into a painful grimace. He finished dressing her as gently as possible before picking up the wig in his trembling hands.

I am a fool. No, fool wasn't a strong enough word. He was a complete and total asshole, a man so obsessed with bedding her he hadn't been able to connect the dots.

A light sheen of tears stung his eyes. He thought back to everything he knew about her, from the loss of her parents to putting up with the prick who had treated her so badly. And he remembered the night he'd followed her, and her reluctance to accept his offer. She hadn't wanted to burden him, even at the risk of her own health.

She carried the load of her illness all by herself. How many people could have done what she was doing? Not many. In that moment, Ryker not only saw her as the woman he was attracted to... he saw her for who she really was, and he was awed.

Amanda looked so small and young in the large bed. Much too young to experience the traumatic illness ravaging her body. And as he stared at her bald head and fragile appearance, he wished in the deepest part of his soul that she had been his mate. In all the years of his life, he'd never admired or desired any woman like he did her. He wanted to take the fragile beauty for his own and be her everything.

Is this love? Ryker didn't know. He'd never fancied himself in love before so he had no experience with it. He'd desired and bedded plenty of women, but that had been all he needed or wanted from them. With Amanda, it was different, though. He felt consumed by her. It was a deeply emotional moment for a man who prided himself on having no emotions at all.

Even if it was love, what future could he offer her? *None*, he realized in bleak despair. Amanda wasn't his mate. If he took her, if he offered her the possibility of something long term, one day he'd have to hurt her. It was a lot of ifs—especially considering their current situation.

The front door of his home opened and closed before footsteps rushed across the foyer. One, two, three sets of feet raced up his stairs, the others following his scent. Ryker raised his eyes from the wig to the doorway to watch as Doctor Sanders rushed in, quickly followed by Alexander and then Marrok.

The doctor immediately started to examine Amanda's unconscious body, a stethoscope in his hand. The other two men looked solemn, but it was Alexander's eyes that held Ryker's attention. In them he saw pity and compassion, and for some odd reason it touched him.

Doctor Sanders stopped long enough to jerk his head toward the open doorway. "I need the three of you to wait outside. *Now.* It's best if I examine her without any distractions. When I'm done, you'll be the first to know, but for now there is no time for delays."

Reluctantly, Ryker led the other men out. Turning his back on her helpless form to walk away was one of the hardest things he'd ever done. He didn't recognize the man he was becoming, but it was what it was. Like it or not, he was emotionally invested in her fate. What happened to her mattered.

Marrok closed the door behind him. Ryker walked across the hallway to the opposite wall before sinking down on the floor to rest against it. With his eyes closed, he gestured toward the two seats next to him. "They are all yours, if you want them." Whether they stood or sat, he couldn't have cared less. All he wanted was to be left alone with his thoughts.

To his surprise, Alexander slid down to sit next to him. The floor wasn't the place he would have expected the king to sit, but it was where the king clearly wanted to be. Marrok remained standing next to the closed door, his dark eyes watching them closely.

"What does this girl mean to you?" Alexander asked outright, grabbing the bull by the horns. "I've never known you to socialize with humans."

Ryker's throat felt frozen. His thoughts and feelings were too new, he needed time to process them. Even then, he wasn't sure he wanted to share them. It wasn't his style. "I hired her to oversee my home," he finally responded, his voice filled with his reluctance to explain.

"I see," Alexander replied. That was exactly what Ryker was afraid of. The other man was no fool. "You know she's not your mate?" Alexander looked off as he said it, as if he hated to say the words.

"I know," Ryker admitted, exhaling loudly. Admitting she wasn't his mate just didn't feel right, but it was the truth. None of it made any sense. *I am seriously fucked up.*

"I'm attracted to her," he explained, but he was certain the other two men had already come to that conclusion. He was glad Alexander had brought Marrok with him, instead of one of the other guardians. Marrok was reliable and trustworthy; Ryker felt certain that anything he said would not be repeated. "But it's nothing more than that." It was a lie, and they all knew it.

Both men stared at the wig in his hands. Ryker hadn't realized he was still holding it. He didn't release it, though. They could draw their own conclusions. Most people usually did.

Alexander was the first to look away. "Why don't you tell us what happened tonight?"

"I'm not even sure I know what happened tonight." Ryker felt as if he'd been blindsided. He was still reeling from it all. "I got back home, and I knew something was wrong. She'd left her purse on the floor by the front door, something she never does. And her scent was off. I'm sure you can smell it." He said the last part as a statement. Both men nodded in confirmation.

"I came upstairs, and I found her by the toilet, completely unconscious. It was clear she was ill. I picked her up and called headquarters." He shrugged. "You know the rest."

"Has she always had that taint in her scent?" Marrok asked him, his deep voice filled with curiosity. "I've never quite scented anything like it before."

"I haven't known her for long, but to answer your question, yes. She's had it for as long as I've known her, but not quite this strong. Originally, I'd thought she'd been poisoned." But now Ryker knew it was much, much worse than that. Doctor Sanders could have easily reversed a poison, but he wasn't so sure the other man had a cure for what he suspected Amanda to have.

Alexander's eyes narrowed on his face as he watched him shrewdly. "What do you mean by originally?"

Doctor Sanders opened the door and stepped out, closing it quietly behind him. "He means she has cancer," he informed them, his expression grave. "Isn't that right, Ryker?"

All of the air seemed to flee his lungs at the doctor's words. He'd suspected, but he'd hoped that somehow, someway, he was wrong. He came to his feet. "How bad is it?" Ryker asked, tormented by the confirmation.

The doctor shook his head regretfully. "I never thought I'd say this, but you've actually managed to bring me a patient with a condition I really have no experience in." He paused as if to consider his next words.

"The best I can tell, she's been undergoing chemo and radiation," he mused out loud, his forehead puckered into a frown. "I can smell both of them in her body, but the chemo seems stronger, as if she's had it for a longer duration. And then there's the port, which is usually used in cases like these. She's severely dehydrated, which has caused her current state. I'm not sure if she just wasn't capable of consuming the fluids that she needed or if someone simply forgot to explain how essential they are. Without them, her body is incapable of flushing out the toxins from her treatments. Regardless of the reason though, I've ran an IV line into her arm, and she's getting them now."

"What kind of cancer do you think she has?" Alexander asked quietly, taking a look at Ryker's face. He then grimaced. *I must look pretty bad,* Ryker thought. It couldn't be anywhere near as bad as he felt, though.

"Without seeing test results, I can't say with a certainty. The intestinal area is quite intricate, and cancer can attack just about any part of it. Relying on my wolf senses, though, I'm fairly certain she has cancer of the pancreas."

Doctor Sanders met Ryker's eyes, his expression grave. "It's advanced, son, and the prognosis doesn't look good. Pancreatic cancer is one of the deadliest forms, and the survival rate is extremely low. Maybe her doctors know something I don't, being that they specialize in these types of conditions, but I just wanted to give it to you straight."

"So this is how they treat it?" Ryker burst out, frustrated beyond belief. "They essentially poison their patients in the hopes of killing it out?"

"Cancer is hard to beat," Doctor Sanders replied. "It's one of those diseases that exists only to kill off its host. And it's quite effective in its job. There aren't a lot of options available, unfortunately."

Ryker didn't immediately respond. He was aware of the other men's scrutiny, but he didn't care. Mate or not, he couldn't just let her die. "What if I changed her?" he asked quietly, the idea growing on him by the second. He'd never changed a human before, but then again, there had never been a reason to.

"And what if she despised you for it?" Alexander interrupted, vehemently shaking his head. "And that's if it even worked. She's not of our world, and I'm willing to bet she has no idea that werewolves even exist. Who's to say that she'd even want to be one? And if you told her, you'd have no choice but to change her. We can't have humans running around with that kind of knowledge."

"I couldn't give a shit less," Ryker roared out, his eyes blazing. "At least she'd still be alive."

"Alive for what, though?" Alexander asked him, but he wasn't unkind. "It's clear you have a romantic interest in her, but what about when you meet your mate? When you do, you'll have no choice but to claim her. And speaking from experience, once you're mated you'll have no thoughts of any other woman, I can guarantee you that. Anything you might have shared with Amanda won't mean anything. It would devastate her."

He stood up to face Ryker, his expression set. "The final decision rests on your shoulders, but I urge you to think long and hard on this before acting. There is no middle ground. If you tell her about us, you will have to change her. It's not a decision you want to take lightly."

Chapter 8

Amanda rolled over in the bed, her eyes opening to reveal the weary man sitting in the chair next to her. She stared at him blankly for a moment—wondering why he was in her room—before groaning. *Clearly, he found me and carried me to bed.*

She felt a tug in her arm as she moved it. A needle was taped into her arm. It was connected to a bag hanging from the headboard. Someone had inserted it, but why couldn't she remember? "Why do I have an IV?"

"You were dehydrated," Ryker explained, with an odd note that Amanda couldn't place. "I found you passed out on the floor, so I called a doctor. He came and treated you."

"Okay," Amanda replied, bewildered by the way he was acting. Her body was filled with dread over his behavior. Something was bad wrong, she just didn't know what. "I didn't know they still made house calls."

"They don't usually, but I know this one personally. That's not really important, though." Ryker paused for a moment before asking, "Why didn't you tell me?"

She stared at him in confusion. He slowly extended his hand, his eyes locked on her face. Amanda gasped when she saw the wig in his hand. Raising her free hand to her head she touched the surface, confirming what she already knew. *Bald.*

Dear God, what am I going to do now?

"I'll be out today," Amanda said immediately, looking away from him in humiliation. It was all too much. The attraction she felt for him only made her unattractiveness hurt her even more. Everything about Ryker was completely perfect, while everything about her was just so wrong. Even on her best days, a man like him would never give a woman like her the time of day. To her horror, her eyes watered up with tears. *Great.*

"Absolutely not." His voice left no room for argument. "Why on earth would you even want to?"

"I can't talk about this right now," she replied, breathing carefully through her mouth. Amanda was fighting to stay in control over her emotions. He was making it very difficult. "Can you please call the doctor and ask him to remove this? We'll talk after he's done."

He has to leave. Her control was slipping, and she needed time to process it all. She felt raw with pain. There was no hiding her condition, and the consequences of that were brutal. She'd never wanted him to see her as she really was. She'd only wanted him to see her at her best. It was too late for that now.

She expected him to leave. After all, what person would stay? So, she was completely stunned when she felt the bed dip down beside her. Instantly, she was wrapped in the scent that was only his, as he gently turned her face towards him.

"I'm not leaving," he informed her, his blue

eyes serious as he looked into hers. "And neither are you. Even contemplating such a thing is insane. There's no reason for you to leave."

It was hard for Amanda to think, with his body pressed so closely to hers. Cancer or not, she wasn't immune to his sensuality. She blinked rapidly in a desperate attempt to hold back her tears. She wasn't one to cry in front of other people. "This isn't a random illness," she explained to him, her voice hoarse from the pain of holding in her emotions. "I have to take chemo every other week. Yesterday, they added on radiation, and it has made me a lot sicker. How on earth could I ask anyone to take something like this on? I can't." She stopped to shake her head, hoping he understood.

"You're not asking. I'm demanding." Ryker released her face, but he didn't leave her side. "Having you here has been a huge relief, and I'm not just saying that. The cook and maids now have someone else to check in with besides me." He shot her an irresistible grin. "How am I supposed to plan a weekly menu? Do I look like the type of guy who wants to oversee that part of the household? I'm just a man. I like to eat the food, not be involved in its planning."

He had a point. With his build and sheer masculinity, Ryker would be more at home outside of the confines of a house. *Like in the woods naked, with his gorgeous body illuminated in the moonlight.*

"Don't you have a girlfriend?" She had to know. It was impossible to believe that any man that looked like him could be single.

"No, and I'm not looking for one. So that is not an issue," he said rather abruptly. Was it a warning? Amanda decided to change the subject.

"I don't really have any family," she confessed to him, her voice low. She looked down at her arm, in the pretense of adjusting her line. "My parents died in New York when the planes crashed into the twin towers. I have an older sister, but we aren't close. I guess our personalities are too different."

"I lost my parents at a young age, too," he confided. "I didn't have any siblings, though."

"I've got pancreatic cancer," she continued in a conversational tone. Amanda had to distance herself away from her condition, or she would have never been able to get through explaining it. "It's considered to be one of the most lethal cancers. It's a fluke that I've got it. As far as I know, nobody in my family ever had cancer. At first I thought it was acid reflux. When it started feeling like someone had punched me in my esophagus, I knew it was something worse. I never dreamed it would be something this bad, though."

Ryker listened to her silently. "I-I don't know how long I'll be here," she informed him. "That's why I told you I couldn't stay longer than a month or two. My doctor is only concerned with keeping me alive as long as possible, in the hopes that one day soon a newer, more effective treatment will become available."

The hand that rested on his thigh clenched, but

otherwise he didn't respond. The silence was unnerving, so she continued to talk. "I'm not sure if it's this way for everyone, but my reaction to the treatments seem to be pretty severe. If I stay, I will be like this every other week. I would imagine it won't be like this forever." It couldn't be. She'd either die or make a recovery.

"Would it make you feel better if I just tossed you out on your ass?" Ryker asked blandly. "If so, I'm afraid you're going to be rather disappointed." He came to his feet before placing the wig on the comforter, next to her.

His black eyebrows pulled together as he stared down at her. "Now that I'm aware of your medical condition, there will be some changes around here. For starters, I will be accompanying you to your next treatment."

Amanda started to protest, but he held up his large hand to stop her. "No arguments," he informed her, his voice curt. "It's ridiculous that you've been driving yourself anyhow. Is your doctor aware of this little fact?"

She looked away before shaking her head. "I didn't think so," he said, making a small noise of disapproval. "Well, it won't be an issue anymore. I have quite a deal of leniency with my position, so leaving work will not be a problem. I've also consulted with the doctor that treated you last night, and he is looking into new treatment options. Doctor Sanders has a good deal of connections, if anyone can find something more effective it would be him."

Ryker started to pace, reminding her of a tiger in a cage. The movements of his lean body were perfectly coordinated, he didn't just walk, he glided. "In the meantime, though, you're going to take much better care of yourself. You need to eat often to build your strength up, and you need more sleep. There really is no reason for you to work, not anymore."

"No," Amanda cut him off. "I won't quit my job, at least not right now. Regardless of what you might think, I do need to work. I don't expect you to fully support me. God knows you've done enough already. If the time comes that I can no longer work then I will just have to let it go, but that time isn't here yet."

Unfortunately, it probably wouldn't be until she was dead. The medical bills were mounting by the day. It looked like she'd have to go another year without air conditioning in her car, but there was no help for it. There was only so much she could do with an empty wallet, and luxuries like air conditioning simply weren't a consideration.

But Ryker didn't need to know those things. He'd done too much for her already. In fact, the man had been a blessing. She was grateful for everything. "Thank you," she told him, her voice filled with sincerity.

"For what?" Ryker stared down at her, a bemused expression on his attractive face.

"For finding me in the woods that night and

allowing me to stay here. You've been kind, much too kind, especially considering I'm a stranger, and I come with a lot of baggage. I just wanted you to know I appreciate it."

Her words seemed to please him, but he didn't say so. "I'm going downstairs to call Doctor Sanders and let him know you're awake. Do you need me to assist you to the facilities before I go?"

Amanda flushed scarlet as she shook her head. She was certain she could make it by herself, but holding her bag of fluids would be a bit tricky. Although weak and shaky, she felt a great deal better than she had the day before. She'd manage. She always did.

"Just holler if you need anything," he told her, turning toward the door. "Otherwise, I'll be back in fifteen minutes."

* * * * *

Amanda handed the customer his change before clearing a few empty mugs and bottles off of the bar. It was her first night back to the Red Ruby since receiving radiation, and she was doing all right. *So far, so good.* And it was all due to Ryker.

It was another busy weekend night, made more so by the live band Jean had hired to play. Amanda took the next customer's order, but her thoughts weren't on the halfway inebriated male that stood in front of her. Instead, she thought of Ryker.

He'd arranged for the doctor to come back. After examining her, Doctor Sanders declared her to be well enough to have the IV removed, much to Amanda's relief. She'd always hated needles, and the port line had been bad enough.

She hadn't thought to ask him why he hadn't used the port, but it really didn't matter. Her latest crisis was over, and overall she felt pretty good. She was a little weak and tired, but not enough to send her home. Of course she still had several hours until closing time. By then, it might be a different story.

"How are things going?" Jean asked her, moving over to stand next to the cash register. The older woman looked well. In fact, she looked happier than she had in a long, long time. Amanda was sure it had something to do with the gentleman she was seeing. There was nothing that could brighten a woman's day faster than a new love interest.

"Good, I suppose," Amanda replied, smiling at her customer as she took his money. Turning she rang it up on the cash register before placing it in the tray.

"I've hired on a new bartender," Jean informed her, patting her gently on the arm. "And I trained her while you were off. She's a college student, so she's not looking for anything more than part time. You're still my full-time bartender, but if you need some extra time off, don't hesitate to ask. Brandy said she is available just about any time, so long as it's in the evenings."

"That's good to know," Amanda replied solemnly. "Thank you for being so nice about all of this."

"Oh, of course," Jean exclaimed, her eyes wide. "It's no problem at all. You've been an excellent employee for all of these years, it's nice to give a little something back."

"I'm no longer living with Jimmy," Amanda informed her, drying her hands on a towel. "We've split up. It happened a few weeks ago, but I needed some time to deal with it in my own mind before telling anyone else about it. He's got another woman living with him now."

Jean shocked her with her response. "Good for you," she told Amanda, her eyes filled with approval. "He was never good enough for you anyhow, and you are well rid of him."

"Really?" Amanda paused to stare at her, her voice filled with disbelief. "I thought you liked Jimmy."

"No, you liked him," Jean corrected her. "And you were the one that imagined herself to be in love with him. So I had to accept that, all the while praying that one day you'd see him for the self-centered little prick he really is. I like you, Amanda. There was no way I would have alienated you by putting down your choice of boyfriend. But now that you're rid of him, I can finally say my piece. I've always believed you've deserved much better than him. And maybe now you've finally got a chance of getting it."

"I'm actually happier since we have split up, believe it or not."

"You certainly look it," Jean shot back, but

then she frowned before asking, "Where are you living at now?"

The glass door to the bar opened wide, revealing the extremely tall male that stood in the doorway. He wore a black shirt and matching jeans, the material clinging to his skin just enough to reveal his hard, muscular frame. His blue eyes searched the room before landing on Amanda. Her fingers fluttered nervously as their eyes connected, the mug in her hand slipping out of her shaky grip. It dropped to the floor before shattering into a million pieces. Amanda barely noticed. Ryker was sexy as hell... and she was tempted enough to sin.

Jean jerked out of the way. "Are you all right?" she asked Amanda in a concerned voice, taking her arm to get her attention.

"Him," Amanda replied dazedly, watching as Ryker advanced. "I'm living with him."

"Sweet Jesus," Jean breathed out as she turned to see who Amanda was looking at. "No wonder you dropped the mug," she added knowingly, a pleased expression on her face. "I probably would have dropped a lot more than that, including my panties."

She let go of Amanda's arm just a second before Ryker reached them. Leaning close to Amanda she whispered, "Isn't it just amazing how things work out sometimes? When one door closes, another one always opens. I told you there would be someone else. You just had to knock down that wall first."

Jean turned away just as Ryker leaned over the

bar. Amanda barely noticed. His scent washed over, pulling her in. It was masculine and woodsy, just like the man. What would he smell like directly from his skin? Heat invaded her, nearly burning her alive in its intensity.

"I'll be back," Jean said over her shoulder, grinning when Amanda's stunned eyes swung in her direction. "I'm going to grab the broom and the dust pan. Don't let Amanda pick up that glass," she warned Ryker. "I don't want her to get cut."

"Yes, ma'am," Ryker drawled out, winking at Amanda. Ever since he'd found out about her cancer, she'd been spending quite a bit of time with him. Although she was seriously attracted, she enjoyed the friendship that had developed between them. It was nice.

"What are you doing here?" she asked him, a breathy note in her voice. She hoped he wouldn't notice.

Ryker shrugged before glaring at the man seated next to him. After a moment, the guy hopped off of the bar stool, quickly disappearing into the crowd. He didn't look back. *Weird.*

Taking the now empty seat, Ryker grinned mischievously. "I heard there was a live band, so I thought I'd come up to have a few beers."

Amanda smiled back, powerless to resist. He was an extremely charming man. "In that case, I better get busy. You want a bottle or a draft?"

"The usual," he replied, pulling his wallet out.

"This one is on me," Amanda told him, taking a frosted mug out of the freezer. "It's the least I can do."

Grabbing a coaster, she placed it in front of him. Jean came back with the broom and dust pan. Taking it from her, she bent over to clean up her mess. "I'm so sorry about dropping that," she told the other woman, sweeping the shards into the dust pan.

"Nonsense," Jean waved her apology away. "It's a bar, glass gets broken all the time around here."

She had a point there. Even the front door had been replaced several times but that had been due to fights. She'd seen several of them over the years. It was to be expected, considering where she worked.

Finished with sweeping, Amanda carried the broom and dustpan to the back room. When she returned, she waited on several customers. It was amazing how quickly people could drink. The beer flowed like water, which was a good thing. Jean was going to be very pleased.

The other woman deserved it. With the economy being as bad as it was, it had hurt the bar, too. Business was increasing, though, and it looked like the Red Ruby was making a comeback. Bringing in a band had been a very wise thing to do.

Surprisingly, Ryker remained where he was. He didn't make any attempt to leave his seat, but he did turn to the side to watch the band. At the next lull, Amanda went over to talk to him.

He noticed her immediately. Unlike a lot of

men, Ryker was always in tune with his surroundings. He wasn't the type of man to constantly play with his cell phone. His manners were impeccable, and Amanda admired that. It was a little off-setting when someone found their phone more interesting than the people around them. Amanda should know. Jimmy had adored his.

His eyes traveled across her face, his expression unreadable. Amanda knew it was impossible, but it felt like a touch. *A very enjoyable touch.*

"You look nice tonight," he told her, his husky voice making her shiver. "Are you feeling better?"

"Much," Amanda replied, but her voice quivered. Ryker was *potent*. There wasn't a moment she wasn't aware of her extreme attraction to him, and the pressure only continued to build. She was going to make a fool out of herself, she just knew it.

"You know, you don't have to stay here by me." She cleared her throat nervously. "I don't want you to feel like you have to babysit me. You'd probably have a better time at one of the tables. I won't be offended if you want to move over."

"I'm fine where I'm at, but I wouldn't mind another draft."

Amanda smiled. Secretly, she was glad he didn't want to move. She filled his mug and brought it back to him before walking away. It would be too easy to get used to him being there.

The crowd was loud and boisterous. Everyone

appeared to be having a good time, and there hadn't been any fights. After midnight, the crowd thinned a bit. The tips were great, but she was tired. In between drink orders she washed mugs, trying to get an early start on closing up. They had to be cleaned in preparation for the next day.

Someone moved in front of her. A woman giggled, but it wasn't pleasant. It had a malicious edge that Amanda didn't like. She looked up to find Jimmy staring at her, with an arm wrapped around his new girlfriend. He stared down at Amanda mockingly, while Bobbi popped her bubblegum. She all but rolled her eyes. Clearly, he'd come to the bar to gloat. It was bound to happen, sooner or later.

Drying her hands on a dishrag, she asked, "What can I get you?"

"We'll take two beers and bring us some frosted mugs. Does that sound good, baby?" Jimmy watched Amanda while he nuzzled the other woman's neck. *If he's waiting for a reaction, he's going to be sadly disappointed.* All she felt for him was disgust.

Amanda turned away, not waiting to hear Bobbi's response. The sooner they had their beers, the sooner she wouldn't have to deal with them. Carrying the bottles in one hand and the mugs in the other, she set them down on the bar as she waited for Jimmy to pay.

He took his sweet time before pulling out some money. "I don't like the looks of that mug," he complained, pointing at the one directly in front of him. "It doesn't look clean."

There was nothing wrong with it, but Amanda gave him a replacement. He was in one of his mean moods; she could see it from a mile away. But he wasn't her problem anymore. By kicking her out, he'd actually done her a favor. She pictured thanking him for it and almost laughed out loud.

Jimmy picked up one of the beer bottles and sampled it, the money clasped tightly in his hand. "This beer isn't cold," he spat out, his upper lip curled up in disgust. "Is this your petty way of trying to get back at me, just because I dumped your sorry ass?"

His words embarrassed her, but she was determined not to show it. Lifting up the bottle, she felt the bottom. It was ice cold. "There's nothing wrong with this beer," she told him dismissively, refusing to give him the satisfaction of acknowledging the rest of his statement. "It's as cold as they come. You need to pay me; I've got other customers who are waiting for drinks."

Jimmy refused to let it go. He was angered by her lack of response to his new girlfriend, and he wanted to make a scene. Amanda stared at him in disgust. *How was I ever interested in a man like him?* Physically, Jimmy was attractive, but what was underneath—the important stuff—was seriously lacking.

"Jean," Jimmy roared, his face red with anger. He didn't have to wait long. The other woman was already making her way over to them.

"Is this the kind of service you're giving your paying customers now?" he asked, when she stopped next to Amanda. "As I'm sure you've heard, I broke up with Amanda. Apparently, she thinks she can pay me back by serving up dirty glasses and warm beer. She needs to grow up. Maybe if she worked on bettering herself, some man might actually want her." He smirked in Amanda's direction, certain Jean would reprimand her.

Ryker stepped up to the bar, using his large frame to push past Jimmy. When he did, the other man almost fell over. Jimmy glared up at him with a disgusted look on his face, but he kept his mouth shut.

Ryker leaned across the bar, with a flirtatious expression on his clean-shaven face. He was only inches away, so close she could have kissed him. "How much longer do you have to be here, baby?" he asked her, his posture relaxed and easy. "I can't wait to get you back home." He wiggled his eyebrows suggestively, his meaning clear to all of them.

"I-uh," she stammered out, but Ryker didn't give her time to finish. He pressed his lips to hers and suddenly none of it mattered.

Raw need slammed into her at the first taste. As if they had a mind of their own, her hands shot out and wrapped around the back of his head, marveling at the softness of his hair. She couldn't get enough. Her desire grew, heat flooding the center of her body. It was easily the most intense kiss of her life.

Ryker pulled slowly away. His eyes were wide

open and filled with heat. He'd watched her the entire time they kissed. Amanda trembled, attempting to remind herself it was all just an act. Her body didn't seem to care.

"What?" Jimmy shrieked, in an incredulous tone of voice. They all turned to look at him, even Ryker. Jimmy shook his head in disbelief as he pointed at her. "You're a real piece of work, Amanda. Do you really expect me to believe that a man who looks like this would really want your fat ass?"

That was all he got out. One moment Jimmy was standing there, but the next he was flat on his back. Ryker had punched him and Jimmy landed on a table, breaking it in the process. He was knocked out cold.

Ryker stared at him, a pleased expression on his face. He turned back to face Jean and pulled out his wallet. "Let me pay you for that table, and don't worry. I'll take the trash out," he said conversationally, placing the money in front of her. "Somehow, a hundred doesn't seem like enough. I would have paid a lot more for the opportunity to punch him out." Jean took the money, with a flabbergasted expression on her face.

By the time Ryker reached Jimmy, the other man was stirring. He picked him up with one hand, dragging him toward the door. Using his other hand to hold it open, he tossed him out into the parking lot.

Bobbi ran past him, screaming Jimmy's name. Ryker ignored her, his attention focused on the cowering male in front of him. "Don't ever let me here you talk to Amanda like that again," he warned him, his deep voice loud enough for Amanda to hear it. Jimmy glared up at him from the ground, holding a hand to his nose. "Next time I won't be so nice. If I were you, I'd make sure my ass was well away from here before I come back out this door with the table. I might decide that one punch wasn't enough, not for the shit you were saying to her."

Sobbing, Bobbi pulled at Jimmy until he came to his feet. He glared at Ryker and then Amanda before allowing her to lead him away. Ryker let the door close with a resounding bang.

Chapter 9

Amanda drove home that night, marveling at how bright everything seemed to be. The moon seemed to illuminate the world in a way she hadn't seen before. It was magical, but so was her kiss from Ryker. No matter what she did, she couldn't seem to push it from her thoughts. Amanda was consumed by it.

She pulled into the driveway, humming to herself. Turning her headlights off, she sat in the car and laughed. Watching Jimmy fly across the room had startled her, but she couldn't deny experiencing just a small bit of satisfaction at seeing him put in his place. It was bad enough he cheated on her and dumped her for another woman, but coming into the bar in an effort to get her fired was too much. Maybe he'd finally learned his lesson, but she doubted it. She shook her head in bemusement as she climbed out of the car.

The sky wasn't as dark as it had been when she'd left the bar. Dawn was quickly approaching. She'd had to work past her usual shift, and Amanda was beat. She couldn't wait to shower off the bar smell and climb into the luxurious bed in her room. *And dream of my irresistibly attractive roommate.*

She walked up the steps, her thoughts on Ryker. To her surprise the door opened, revealing the man himself. Her pulse rate increased as she stared at him, soaking in his handsome good looks.

Ryker stepped back to hold the door open.

"Hi," Amanda said nervously, walking inside. Her voice sounded just a tad too chirpy to be natural, especially considering how late it was. "I didn't expect you to be up."

"Why not?" he asked her, his tone amused. "I often keep unusual hours," he continued, his hooded eyes sliding over her body. "Especially when there's an incentive."

Amanda gawked at him, her own eyes raking over his tightly muscled body. *Is he flirting with me?* She found it hard to believe. It was more likely he was being friendly. In a roundabout way, she was his employee. Not to mention the hundred other reasons why he wouldn't be interested.

After examining and discarding several responses, she finally asked, "Did you need to see me about something?"

Ryker closed the door before taking her by her arm. "Actually, there's something I want to show you," he drawled in a deep voice, leading her to the back of the house. He opened the back door and escorted her out onto the deck before speaking again. "Have a seat."

Amanda was completely puzzled by his words and actions, but she did what he asked. Sinking down into the deep cushioning of the sectional sofa she sighed. It felt like paradise to her weary body. Ryker joined her, sliding an arm to rest casually along the back edge of the seat. And in that moment, her night felt complete.

He reached forward to hand her a glass from the rectangular-shaped table in front of them. She took it from him, her heart pounding. He'd planned for her to join him, it was clear from his actions and the platter of food in front of them. Why? Her eyes slid up to his face in question.

Ryker stared right back at her. "The sunrise is one of the best features of this place," he told her softly, silkily, his deep voice washing over her like a sensual touch. "And I wanted you to see it."

Amanda didn't reply. She just continued to stare at him, raw and unfettered need building within her by the moment. His face was so close to hers, his firm lips enticing and begging to be kissed. And in those silent seconds they opened up the door to an erotic awareness that they could no longer ignore.

The silence was broken up only by a small, broken moan of surrender. Or was it unrelenting need? Belatedly, Amanda realized the noise came from her. Ryker was slowly lowering his lips, his heated blue eyes locking her into place for his pleasure. She couldn't have turned away, even if she wanted to. Heat sizzled within her body, concentrating in her breasts and the area between her thighs. She'd left the point of no return a long time before. Her body demanded she have him, in the most basic and physical way possible.

He is treading on dangerous ground, Amanda thought to herself, an instant before he claimed her lips. She couldn't ever recall being so aroused in her life. Sexually, she'd never been the aggressive one, but something about him pushed her pass all of her limits.

* * * * *

At the first taste of her plump lips, blood slammed into Ryker's shaft. He was consumed by lust, the last bit of his restraint and control gone. Never had he desired any female more than he did Amanda. He had to have her.

She moaned against his lips. Ryker smiled at her visible sign of surrender. She wanted, needed, his body as much as he did hers. His lips broke away from hers before taking a slow path down her chin and neck, suckling at her sweet flesh as he went.

He took a deep breath of her scent, disregarding the illness he could still smell within her. *Mine*, he growled in his mind, although he knew it wasn't completely true. For a moment, he was filled with regret, but he couldn't sustain the thought. Not with the scent of her arousal beating at his senses, and the feel of her lush body against his.

Amanda's hands slid along his shoulders, filling him with pleasure. "Touch me," he encouraged her, his voice gruff. "I want to feel your hands *everywhere*." Even the wolf within him seemed to enjoy it, which was odd, considering she wasn't his mate. Generally, when Ryker seduced a woman the wolf remained indifferent—revealing neither approval nor disapproval of his conquests.

Ryker leaned back against the cushions, pulling Amanda across his lap and positioning her with a knee on each side of his hips and thighs. Not giving her time to protest he pulled her face back down to his, kissing her long and leisurely. The heat between her legs rubbed against his shaft through his jeans. She was killing him, but what a way to go.

Whether she planned it, or just the sensuality of their embrace drove her to it, her hips began to move. Ryker's legs stiffened underneath her body as he fought to hold onto his control, but it was a losing battle. "Fuck it," he muttered out, his face against her breasts. "You're driving me wild." He'd take it slow another time.

His fingers seemed to fly as he undid the buttons of her shirt, revealing her large but perky breasts underneath. The air deflated from his lungs. "Gorgeous," he muttered, leaning forward to unclasp the back of her bra. "Simply gorgeous."

And they were. Pushing the shirt off her shoulders and discarding it on the ground, he hooked his trembling fingers underneath her bra straps and slowly eased them off. And when the material fell away, completely exposing her large nipples, Ryker was lost.

Pressing his face close to her chest, he captured one pink tip in his mouth. Amanda groaned, her fingernails digging into his shoulders hard enough to break the skin. *Pleasure and pain.* It only added to his need.

His fingers moved to the waistband of her jeans. "Baby, I can't wait," he told her, almost regretfully. He was somewhat ashamed by his lack of control. "I want you so bad. Your body makes me crazy." He leaned back from her chest to meet her eyes. "So I hope you're as ready as I am because *you're as good as had.*" His voice was confident, much to his surprise.

* * * * *

Amanda stared at him, incoherent with need. His words had been spoken casually, lazily even, but there was nothing casual about his heated eyes and seduction. His fingers expertly undid her button and zipper and were pushing at her jeans. At the rate he was going, he would have her undressed in seconds. It wasn't fast enough. Not even knowing the port was exposed and visible bothered her. She'd never wanted anything more than she wanted him.

Desire rolled through her. She stood up and shoved her jeans down before kicking them away. Ryker growled his approval as he stared at every inch of her, his eyes locking on the area between her legs. Amanda was all but dripping with need. For once in her life, she wasn't ashamed to stand naked in front of someone. There was nothing but pure, unadulterated lust on his face. She couldn't deny how much he wanted her, and if a man like him found her *that* attractive, it would have been foolish to feel embarrassed. It awed her.

"What about the cancer?" she asked him hesitantly, hating to take the chance of turning him off. "Are you worried about being exposed to the chemicals in my body?" The doctor had told her it was possible her vaginal fluids contained them. "You'll need to wear a condom. I wouldn't want you to get sick, and I can't risk getting pregnant."

Ryker undid the button of his own pants before lifting his bottom enough to shove them down to his ankles. He kicked them away, but Amanda's focus was on his shaft. "Oh, my God," she muttered, her voice hoarse. Desire nearly dropped her to her knees, but at the same time she felt a small twinge of worry. She had seen it already, but seeing it was a lot different than actually having it inside of her. How could her body ever accept something that large?

Crowned by a huge mushroom-shaped head, his shaft was easily as thick as a water bottle. And it only got bigger at the base. Amanda gawked at him. The man was not only thick, but he was long. Much longer than a beer bottle. Suckling on his shaft would be a challenge, but her mouth watered all the same. *Talk about a tall glass of water.*

He leaned forward, pressing kisses across the base of her stomach. His chin brushed against her nether hairs. Amanda's legs trembled weakly. His face dropped.

"I can't get you pregnant," he growled against the area between her legs. "And I couldn't care less about any possible exposure. The only thing I'm concerned about is pleasing you and this gorgeous body in front of me. Even if it takes me hours, I will satisfy you... and myself in the process."

And with that, his tongue slowly snaked out into her hidden folds, the pleasure indescribable.

* * * * *

Her taste coated his tongue, sweet and thick like honey. Ryker growled again, wanting, needing more. "I could lick you all night," he muttered hoarsely, his cock twitching at the thought. Wrapping his large hands around her hips, he pulled her over to the cushions. Once she was on her back with her legs spread he resumed his attentions, his tongue everywhere. *Licking. Teasing.*

Amanda screamed from pleasure, her hips moving of their own accord. There was nowhere he didn't taste, and he did it eagerly. She worried for his safety, but there was really no need. As a werewolf, none of her treatments could harm him.

He slowly slid one long, thick finger into her body, his tongue darting rapidly against her swollen nub. "So wet," he groaned out, his voice raspy. As impassioned as he was, Ryker was losing control. It showed. His voice sounded more animalistic than human.

Amanda was close to orgasm, he could tell by her flowing juices and the clenching motions of her inner body. He wrapped his free hand around his shaft, gripping it tightly as he fought to hold back. He was so aroused he had to have the pressure; he feared he'd lose control just from watching her come.

"Release for me, sweetheart," Ryker murmured against her silken folds. "I want to taste you on my tongue."

His words propelled her over the edge. Her feline-like moans were the sweetest thing he'd ever heard, but they crazed him. He had to be inside her.

His release was lodged in his balls, his shaft burning with need. With the grace of an animal he slid over her, supporting his weight with his hands. Amanda stared up at him, her cheeks pink from pleasure. "Now, Ryker," she gasped out huskily, spreading her legs open as far as possible.

* * * * *

Still reeling from her orgasm, Amanda watched as Ryker slide between her thighs. *Finally.* She felt as if she'd waited for a lifetime for this moment. Nothing mattered to her but having him. Not even his extremely-large shaft could dampen her need. Not since he'd licked her like there was no tomorrow. The pleasure she'd found on his perfect tongue was addictive. Now, she craved every hot, hard inch.

She was too impatient to wait. Reaching between their bodies, she grasped his swollen cock before rubbing it against her blood-engorged slit. Her exhaustion was gone. She was energized, her entire body on the very edge of some unknown edge of pleasure that confounded her. Somehow, Ryker was the key to it. In his arms, she found a pleasure she'd only read about in romance novels. And now she wanted to finish it.

His shaft was hard and heavy in her hand. Ryker grasped her by her hips, lifting her up enough to slide a cushion underneath. It brought them even closer together. "Show me how much you want me," he gently goaded her, flexing his hips enough to make his cock press against her core. Amanda gasped, but Ryker's reaction was much sexier. He threw his head back, the veins in his neck visible as he fought for control. "I want to see that tight little pussy take it in."

It was all the encouragement Amanda needed. She fed him into her body, writhing from pleasure at the sensation of him inside. It was a tight fit, maybe too tight, but her wetness pulled him in. She wanted him to take control. "I've shown you," she told him boldly. "Now, what are you going to do about it?"

Did I really just say that to him? She had. Her words pushed him over the edge. Poised between her thighs, Ryker was wild and untamed, too ruggedly handsome for words. Thrusting his hips, he jabbed a few more inches into her needy body.

"I'll tell you what I'm going to do," he informed her, his thumb moving to rub against her swollen clit. "I'm going to pump my way in until I have to stop, and then I'm going to give you an orgasm unlike anything you've ever felt before." He leaned forward to tongue at her breasts.

God, I hope so.

Ryker thrust lazily, his hips propelling him in deeper. There was no pain, despite her trepidation. It was impossible to think with his scent surrounding her, his blood-engorged shaft buried deep. All she could do was feel. Amanda held onto him, moving her hips in time to his. She wished it could last forever.

The friction increased as her body started to spiral. His next thrust sent her into bliss. The sun peeked over the horizon just as her world exploded. Ryker increased the speed of his thrusts, and an instant later he groaned as he surged within her. Warmth flooded her quivering folds as he filled her with his release. *Holy shit.* She was never going to be the same again.

A silent moment passed by, then another. Amanda was filled with a joyous exhaustion. She was more exhausted than she'd ever been, but for once in her life she actually felt complete. It was the first time she'd ever had an orgasm from oral sex or intercourse, and it was as earth shattering as she always imagined it to be.

There was so many things she wanted to say. Without a doubt, they'd just complicated their relationship, but she couldn't summon up enough energy to care. There would be time to sort it out later —if it could be sorted.

She was determined to enjoy the moment. Looking past Ryker, she marveled at the beauty of the sunrise and the rose-colored skies. Even if she saw a thousand of them, none of them could have ever compared to that one.

Ryker lifted his head from her neck to slowly pull out, his face relaxed. He didn't say a word, but he looked satiated. He sat down at her feet on the sectional before lifting her ankles to his lap. It was a quiet, satisfying end to their explosive lovemaking.

Amanda rolled over on her side as she said drowsily, "This was an amazing sunrise, Ryker. We'll definitely have to do this again. Soon."

And then she succumbed to her exhaustion, hoping he'd understand.

* * * * *

What the fuck was I thinking? Ryker wondered to himself as he watched Amanda fall asleep.

He hadn't intended on seducing her, or so he had thought. But if he were honest with himself, what else could he call it? He felt disgusted with his actions. The healthiest human female would have found it taxing enough to bed him, but he hadn't thought twice about taking her. For the first time in his life, true fear washed over him. *What if it was too much?*

Never again, he vowed to himself, coming to his feet to take her in his arms. She didn't wake up, which was a clear sign he'd crossed the line. Amanda was nearly comatose with exhaustion, and Ryker had never been more shamed in his life. He'd done this to her.

He all but ran through the house and into her room before placing her carefully on her bed. He didn't bother to redress her, but he did ease her wig off of her head. He couldn't understand why she even bothered wearing it, in his eyes she was beautiful.

Is she worried that others will make fun of her? The thought filled him with rage. If he had it his way, she'd quit her job and allow him to take care of her. God knew he had enough money to do so. Private doctors, medical treatments, anything she needed. It wouldn't make a dent in his fortune. All he wanted was the chance to explore the powerful attraction between them. He would do anything in his power to make it happen.

Covering her up with her comforter, he plunked down in the cushioned chair next to the bed. After a moment, he buried his face into his hands. *Should I call the doctor at Wolf Town?* Lifting his head to stare at her lifeless form, he felt as if he had little choice.

He ran back downstairs to grab their clothing and his phone, his thoughts heavy. *What is it about Amanda that pulls me in so deeply?* Ryker felt like he was on a roller coaster, the constant highs and lows keeping him off-balance. The thought of her dying was like a punch in the gut. He felt as if he couldn't even breathe.

What in the hell am I doing? He'd started something between them, something that could never last. And what would he do if his mate just happened to come along? How could he expect her to watch him consumed by lust and passion for another woman, especially while fighting for her own life? Ryker started back into the house, feeling shittier than ever. No matter what happened, someone would be hurt. Him, if she died, or her, when he found his fated female.

Had Amanda been his mate, none of their

problems would be an issue. He could have claimed her and changed her, eradicating the cancer completely. As his mate, she would have had to accept her new life. Wolf Town was full of human mates. They'd all adapted. Amanda would have, too, in time.

She makes me happy. Taking care of her fulfilled some unknown need in him. Never would he have expected to feel so strongly about any female, especially someone he wasn't mated to. The depth of feelings between mates was said to be incomparable, but so were his feelings for Amanda. Ryker shook his head in bemusement, imagining a future spent writing poetry, shopping, and watching chick flicks. If he got any more emotional than he currently was, he'd probably be wearing skirts and pantyhose.

Racing back up the stairs and into her room, he threw their clothing into the nearest chair before dialing the number for headquarters. "Headquarters," a smooth male voice said perkily. "How can I help you?"

Shit. It was Connor, a werewolf known for his mischievous tendencies. Ryker rolled his eyes as he said gruffly, "It's Ryker. Transfer me to the doctor."

"Well, good morning to you, sunshine," Connor retorted. "And why do you need a doctor? You sound like your normal asshole self to me. You know, there are things you can use for your condition. I've heard prune juice and laxatives work miracles."

I am going to kill him. "Put. The. Doctor. On. *Now,*" he roared into the phone, wishing Connor was close enough to grab. "I've got an emergency, and I don't have time for your stupid antics."

"I'll just bet you do," Connor said knowingly. "Buy a bottle of laxatives and read the directions. Take triple, no, four times the recommended dosage, and call us after you're cleaned out." He muttered something that strangely sounded like, "God help your pipes."

"I'm not going to tell you again," Ryker snapped, his voice cold and filled with the promise of death. "I have an emergency here, and I need to talk to the doctor. I'm not fucking around, Connor. You put him on now, or I'm calling Alexander. You and I will have words. *Soon.*" And likely more than that, especially if the other man's delays put Amanda at risk.

"Well, shit," Connor bit back, his voice sullen. "You don't have to get mean about it. I'm transferring you to Doctor Brown now."

After a moment of silence, the doctor came on the line. "Ryker, is it the human female again?" Doctor Brown asked him briskly, all business. He hadn't personally attended to Amanda before, but it was likely he'd seen the log and notes from the previous visit. The doctors at Wolf Town were careful to keep each other well informed about the health and wellness at their settlement... or anyone affiliated with them.

"Doctor," Ryker said hoarsely, completely taxed by worry for Amanda. "I need you to come and examine Amanda. She's not doing well." He didn't want to say more than that, at least not on the phone.

"What are her symptoms?" The doctor asked, his voice puzzled.

"She's not awake," Ryker told him, staring down at her pale face.

The doctor made an odd noise. "Most people aren't awake at this time of the morning," he informed Ryker dryly. "Especially mortals during the weekends."

"She passed out," he admitted heavily.

"That's different," the doctor responded, his voice alert. "What was she doing before losing consciousness?"

Ryker hesitated for just a moment. His fingers gripped the phone with enough pressure to crush it. Thankfully, he didn't. "We had intercourse. I'm afraid I hurt her."

"Holy shit," Connor said on the line. "You've been having sex with her? Isn't she pretty sick? I mean, really, Ryker. Are you telling us the only female you can get into your bed is one that's nearly dead from a debilitating disease?"

"What?" Ryker roared, holding the phone out in front of him to glare at it. He couldn't believe Connor's audacity. Pulling it back to his ear, he fumed, "What in the hell are you still doing on the line? This is private business, asshole." He was completely furious with the other male. "Hang the damned phone up, you moron. And make sure you keep your big mouth shut. I don't want this blabbed all over Wolf Town."

"Clearly, these lines are not secure," Doctor Brown jumped in, his voice cool. "I'm leaving now, and I'll be there shortly. I assure you that when I return I'll make sure a report is made about our supposedly confidential conversation. I'm sure Alexander will find it quite interesting to know that some of our guardians feel as if they have the right to eavesdrop." Both men immediately heard an audible click as Connor hung up. *Good riddance.*

It didn't take him long to arrive. He quickly examined Amanda, but he didn't ask Ryker to leave. The doctor didn't bother to wake Amanda up. Instead he took her vitals and did a quick examination before motioning for Ryker to follow him out.

"Let's go downstairs," he told Ryker, holding his bag in his hand. Ryker nodded, shutting the door to Amanda's room. He followed him, anxious to hear the doctor's diagnosis. "That girl is exhausted," he informed Ryker, stopping at the base of the stairs, "but it didn't appear that being intimate hurt her. Do you know how far along her cancer is?"

Ryker shook his head. "Maybe you should find out," the doctor advised, his eyebrows raised in emphasis. He looked up at Ryker, a grave expression on his face. "For someone on treatments, the cancer smells pretty invasive. Do you know if her tests are showing any progress?"

"No," Ryker answered, clearing his throat. "She hasn't told me."

"Then maybe you should ask her," Doctor

Brown retorted. "From what I understand, there should have been some type of progress. Pancreatic cancer is one of the deadliest forms, and it's a very hard one to treat. So much so that many victims decide to forgo treatment in lieu of enjoying the best possible quality of life, especially when their cancer is as advanced as hers clearly is."

"What do you mean?" Ryker asked, puzzled by his words. He knew the possibility existed that she wouldn't survive, but with her treatments he'd assumed she had a good chance of beating it.

Doctor Brown shot him a pitying look, but he didn't mince his next words, "What I mean is I can scent the cancer in her lungs and liver. I read the report from last time, and I know it wasn't there before. Her cancer is spreading into her other organs, Ryker, and it's spreading fast." He looked away, as if he hated to continue. "The humans don't have medicine or treatment that can fix that, and neither do we. Of course you could change her, but time is running out for even that. You need to start preparing for her demise. I doubt she'll make it another few months."

Ryker stared at the doctor dumbfounded before turning away to look out the window. *She is dying?* He felt as if his lungs were being crushed. He couldn't breathe. In a choked voice, he asked, "What can I do to help her?"

"Keep her comfortable and well-fed," Doctor Brown immediately advised. "I've heard she works at the bar in town, but even that is too much for her. She needs plenty of rest, Ryker. She doesn't need to be working all night, and if my guess is accurate, she won't be able to for much longer anyhow. I would advise you to refrain from intercourse with her, but I know that's difficult when you hold a deep attraction for a female close to you. You'll have to exercise more restraint than you ever have before, should you take her into your bed. And you'll have to become an expert in the form of lovemaking known as the quickie. In her condition, she will never be able to fully satisfy a male werewolf—especially one in the prime of his life."

Ryker immediately shook his head. "I don't know if I can bed her again, not in her condition," he said softly, completely devastated by the news. "Look what I did to her already."

"I saw no signs that her exhaustion came from intercourse," Doctor Brown reminded him. "And I'm not necessarily telling you not to touch her, although I should. Don't go cold on her, not now. Acting as if you don't want her would only do more damage. Psychologically, it would hurt her, and do you really want to send her from this world feeling rejected? She's at the end of her natural life span, Ryker. She doesn't need any more pain than she already has."

He stopped to sigh. "You've set yourself on a hard road, Ryker, and there are no easy answers. Getting involved with a mortal female is tough, especially when it comes to one that is already ill. Their lifetimes are too short, and they are too prone to death. All I can advise you to do is take each day carefully and prepare yourself for the day when it's all over."

Chapter 10

Several days had passed since the morning she made love to Ryker, but there hadn't been a repeat. If anything, he remained completely remote, at least mentally. Physically, she'd been with him daily, spending more time with the man than she ever had. It wasn't enough, not for her.

"Come over here and sit down," Jean called out, pulling Amanda from her thoughts. "If you clean that bar any more I fear it won't have any polish left to it."

"Sorry," Amanda replied, placing the towel down on the counter. She gave the room a once-over, but it was completely dead. Grateful for the lull before the night crowd, she slid gratefully onto the stool next to Jean.

"What's on your mind?" Jean asked her immediately, her eyes narrowed on her face. "The cancer hasn't worsened, has it?"

"Not that I know of," Amanda informed her, debating about the wisdom of sharing her problems. In the end, she decided not to. "I guess I'm just a little bit tired." It wasn't untrue. She hadn't felt like herself in weeks.

"Huh," Jean said in a vague way, taking a drink from her coffee cup. "There's something I've been wanting to talk to you about. I suppose now is as good of a time as any."

Amanda waited for her to continue. The other

woman looked uncomfortable for a moment, but she didn't let it hold her back. "I've been seeing Pat for awhile, as you already know. Pat is a good man, and I like his company. So much so that I'm starting to think I'm a fool for spending all of my time here. I'd like to cut my hours back, but that's not easy when I'm bartending during the day and doing my bookkeeping at night."

Jean paused to eye Amanda, no doubt checking to see how she was responding to her words. "You know this bar almost as much as I do. How would you feel about becoming my bookkeeper?"

Amanda's first inclination was to accept. The truth was, the bartending job was wearing her down, more so than she'd ever thought possible. And it wasn't just the work. The hours were hard on her, too. "What would the hours be?" she asked Jean cautiously, afraid of getting her hopes up just to have them dashed. "And how many hours a week would you need me?"

Jean thought about it for a moment. "I still want to keep my daytime hours," she mused out loud. "But it wouldn't make a difference if you're here during the day or not. So whatever hours you'd like," she finally told Amanda, beaming broadly. "Which sounds best, afternoons or evenings?"

Amanda was floored, but the idea was growing on her by the second. "I guess afternoons," she told Jean, smiling happily. The position really was a godsend. She'd always been good at math, and working as a bookkeeper wouldn't be as physically taxing as bartending. Plus, she wouldn't have to deal with the jerks.

"That settles it," Jean said decisively, a small smile playing about her lips. "You can come in Monday through Fridays. You won't make as much as you made bartending, but I'm sure you expect that?" Amanda nodded, not minding. She was too happy to care.

"When do you want me to start?"

Jean placed her hand on a stack of papers next to her coffee cup. "As soon as possible, if that's okay with you. I wanted to speak with you first before hiring on another bartender. There's a woman named Misty that worked for me years ago, and she's looking to come back. I think she would be the most reliable, in the past she was always on time. Plus, she won't need any training, and that's a big incentive for me. I'll call her tonight and see when she can start. How does that sound?"

"Wonderful," Amanda replied, her mood lightened. She was troubled by Ryker's behavior, but having a new position made her feel pretty good. "You're not doing this because of my health, right?" she asked Jean, watching her reaction. "I wouldn't want you to create a position just for my benefit."

Jean waved her words away, shaking her head in amusement. "You should know me better than that," she cackled. "God knows I don't part with any more money than I need to." Jean was frugal, but she had to be. It was the only way to keep her business afloat, especially in a town as small as Nashoba.

"So are you and Pat an item now?" she asked Jean, smiling happily. "He must be someone pretty important, if you're willing to cut your hours back."

"I won't marry him," Jean warned her, shaking a finger in her direction. "But I can't deny that I like him. At my age, I didn't expect to find someone again. Pat is my type of guy, though. He's handsome, laid back, and rich as hell. I can't find any reason to complain. Enough about me," she continued. "What about you? How is your new living arrangement working out?"

"Good," Amanda replied, somewhat self-consciously. It was all so new to her, and she wasn't sure of his feelings, which left her on shaky ground. "I told Ryker about my cancer."

"And?" Jean asked, picking up the remote to turn the television off. "What did he say?"

"He is extremely accepting of it. In fact, he has treated me better than I could have ever hoped for. Not only is he giving me free room and board, but he's even had a doctor to come over and check on me." She left out the personal parts. "And now he has volunteered to drive me back and forth to my appointments and treatments."

Jean stared at her, her shrewd eyes scanning her face. "I'm glad to hear that he plans on taking you," she finally said. "I would have offered myself, but I knew you wouldn't have let me. You're an independent one, that's for sure. How did he manage to convince you?"

Amanda sighed, looking down at the bar. "The last treatment was pretty hard on me. The doctor decided I need radiation, so he's added it on. It made me pretty sick, and unfortunately Ryker found me passed out on the floor. He called a doctor, one he knows, and the doctor came out and examined me. He knew right off that I had cancer, and he told Ryker."

"You have been that sick, but you didn't tell me?" Jean asked incredulously, her eyebrows lifted high. "You should have said something," she scolded Amanda. "I know you need the money, and you don't want to cut back on your hours, but there comes a point in life where you have to listen to your body and slow down. You've been working too hard already."

To Amanda's surprise, she smiled. "But you're lucky. Not many women have a handsome man like Ryker to swoop in and make it all better. And he couldn't have come at a better time, huh?"

Jean was right. She didn't know how she'd gotten so lucky. She appreciated him, but her feelings went much deeper than that. But how did he feel about her? He wasn't avoiding her, but he wasn't affectionate, either. Amanda felt as if a wall had been erected between the two of them. By having sex, they'd crossed into previously unexplored territory. Was he was regretting it? Maybe.

The bar door swung open, sunshine pouring into the darkened building. Jimmy stalked in the room, his face red and furious. Spotting the two women, he stormed across to them.

Now what? The two women exchanged a wary look. Jimmy was nothing but trouble. When he got close he held up his hand, reveal several crumpled papers. "You bitch, you just don't know when to stop, do you?"

Amanda stared at him, completely dumbfounded. "I have no idea what you're talking about."

"Yeah, I'm just sure you don't," he jeered back, his lip curled up in dislike. "You won't stop at anything, will you? Since I won't have you, you're going to do everything you can to make my life miserable. I'm going to fight this, Amanda, and everyone is this town is going to see just how pathetic you really are."

"That's enough," Jean burst out, turning around to glare at Jimmy. "This is my damn bar, and I won't put up with you talking to my employee like that. If you've got a problem, you better spit it out quick. You've got about five seconds before I call the sheriff and have your sorry ass hauled over to the jailhouse."

"For what?" Jimmy exclaimed, holding his hands out in puzzlement. "I'm the victim here."

"For pissing me off," Jean shot back, holding her phone in her weathered hand. "Now straighten up and spit it out. I don't have time for this shit. Maury is about to come on, and I'm not missing my show for you."

Jimmy nodded stiffly. Even he wasn't foolish

enough to go against the older woman. He glared at Amanda as he said, "Your little boyfriend bought my place, and now he has served me with an eviction notice, as if you didn't know."

Amanda gaped at him in disbelief. Was it just a coincidence? Somehow she doubted it. She didn't know how or why, but Ryker had done it for her. The man would never cease to amaze her.

With a small smile playing about her lips, she met Jimmy's enraged eyes and said calmly, "How about that? I guess it really is true. What comes around does go around. Tell me, Jimmy, how does it feel? At least you've gotten a warning that you need to move out, which is more than you ever gave me."

He threw the papers down on the nearest table before grabbing up an empty beer bottle and breaking it on the edge of the wood. His face was menacing as he held it up. "Bobbi left me today, all because of you. I should have done a lot more than slap your sorry ass when I threw you out," Jimmy hissed, his body tense. "You're going to call your boyfriend right now and get this dropped, or I'm going to kill you, you jealous bitch."

Amanda stood up. Her hands were trembling, but she wouldn't show her fear. Jimmy was crazed, she didn't doubt for a moment that he was fully prepared to hurt her. In his mind, he believed she was responsible for everything that had gone wrong in his life. He wasn't mature enough to account for his own actions. "You need to leave, Jimmy," she told him, her voice firm. "You need to leave before this gets out of hand, and you do something you'll regret."

Jimmy gave her a cold, cruel smile. "The only thing I regret is ever moving your sorry ass into my home. I cheated on you the whole time I was with you, you know it? It was the only way I could take having you in my house, but I kept you around because you paid the bills. Financially, it benefited me, but I couldn't stand your fat ass. And now, you won't leave me alone, so I'm going to take matters into my own hands. One way or another, you're going to get it through your stupid skull. I'm done with you, bitch."

At that moment, all hell broke loose.

Jean spun around in the bar stool to face Jimmy, her cell phone in one hand and a pistol in the next. She cocked it while pointing it in his direction. He froze, his eyes darting from her face to her hand as if attempting to determine how serious she was. Whatever he saw was enough to convince him. He didn't move.

"Take the phone, honey," she told Amanda, her voice grim. "Call the sheriff and tell him to get his ass over here quick. And if he delays, he better bring an ambulance." She stopped, her eyes narrowing harshly at Jimmy. "I told you, don't nobody come between me and Maury. *Nobody.*"

The bar door swung open. "Freeze," a male voice yelled out. Amanda risked a quick glance, surprised to see the sheriff. Behind him was Ryker, his face hard.

Jimmy turned to look before releasing a disgusted noise from the back of his throat. He dropped the broken beer bottle and turned to fully face the sheriff. "Thank God you're here," he said, grabbing the papers from the table. "As you can see, they were going to kill me. I want them arrested, the both of them."

He started toward the door, but the sheriff's next words stopped him. "Do you got a hearing problem, boy? I said freeze." He stopped to toss a pair of handcuffs at Ryker. "Cuff him up."

Jean slid her pistol back into her purse. "You've got some mighty good timing, sheriff," she told him calmly, coming to her feet. "Another moment or two, and I would have been forced to take matters into my own hands. What kind of beer do you drink? This one is on the house."

To Amanda's surprise, the sheriff accepted her offer. "Shut up, and take a seat," he told Jimmy, climbing up onto a bar stool. He grabbed the beer from Jean and took a long swig from it before adding, "What kind of man goes around threatening women like you just did? I'm of mind to lock you up and throw away the key."

He stopped to chuckle, his expression deeply amused. "And did you ever pick the wrong woman to fuck with. Jean doesn't take any shit." He stopped and jerked his head in Ryker's direction. "You better be damned glad that Ryker called me in time. Otherwise, I would have arrived to find your sorry hide full of bullet holes. It's nothing better than you deserve. I don't have any patience for men like you."

Ryker threw Jimmy into a chair, standing next to him as he held him in place. Jimmy ignored him in favor of watching the sheriff. "I demand to speak to an attorney. I have rights, you know?"

"Not in my town you don't," the sheriff bit back. He turned to look at Jean and Amanda, his expression sincere. "Are both of you ladies all right?"

Amanda nodded, but Jean spoke up. "He came in here causing problems over an eviction notice, something neither one of us knows anything about. This isn't the first time he's been in here harassing Amanda, and I want something done about it."

"Don't you worry about that," the sheriff replied, his voice firm. He finished off his beer before thumping the empty bottle down on the bar. Coming to his feet he walked over to Jimmy, his thumbs looped in his waistband.

"It would seem that you've pissed off a lot of people lately. The way I see it, you came in here with the intent to kill this young lady, and that holds a mighty harsh sentence. Prison is the only way to keep you from troubling these people again. So I'm going to take you in and book you. Problem solved."

"Wait!" Jimmy screamed out, a panicked expression on his face. "She's the one that won't leave me alone. She's mad because I won't take her back. I'm just trying to protect myself from this psycho. You can't put me in prison for that."

"Oh, really?" the sheriff asked dryly, crossing his arms as he stared down at him. "And how exactly has she been bothering you?"

"Amanda put her boyfriend up to evicting me," Jimmy told the sheriff smugly. "It doesn't matter what I do. She'll always find some other way to torment me, just because I broke up with her."

"Is this true, Ryker?" The sheriff looked doubtful.

"I purchased the property that this man lives on. It borders mine. I'm of mind to expand my property line, so I'll be bulldozing the mobile home. I had Jimmy served with an eviction notice, but it was nothing that Amanda was even aware of."

The sheriff smirked. "Well, there is nothing wrong with that. It sounds all legal-like to me," he replied, shrugging his shoulders. "And I don't have time for has-been boyfriends that don't have anything better to do than to make trouble. From the way I see it, this woman has already moved on." He stopped to look between Ryker and Jimmy before shaking his head. "Why would she want shrimp when she can have the whole lobster? Get real, boy."

"What if I agreed to pack up and leave today?" Jimmy asked, in a last-ditch effort to avoid going to jail. "Hell, I'll even leave the state. There's nothing holding me here. Believe me, I couldn't care less if I ever saw any of you again." He added the last part sullenly, in true Jimmy fashion.

The sheriff exchanged a long look with Ryker.

Despite his relaxed attitude, there was nothing lazy about the lawman. He was sharp. If Jimmy thought he could outsmart him, he was in for a huge disappointment.

"What do you think, Ryker?" he drawled, walking in a slow circle around Jimmy's seat. "Do you think he's serious, or is he just trying to pull one over on us?"

"No, I'm serious," Jimmy squeaked out. "Just let me go, and I promise you I'll never step foot in this town again. I've been thinking about leaving anyhow. Bobbi has been asking me to move to Las Vegas. She wants to be a dancer, and that's where the money is. I'm going to follow her out, and see if she takes me back."

"Release him," Ryker said, a hard edge to his voice. After the sheriff undid Jimmy's handcuffs, he yanked him to his feet. "I'm going to let you be, this time. I'm telling you now, though, don't think I'll play nice twice. Get the hell off of my land, and don't make the mistake of coming back. Amanda is done with you, and she has been done with you. Don't let me see you again."

Jimmy held his hands up as he pulled away from Ryker. "Whatever you say, man." He turned and fled, the glass door hitting the wall outside. A few seconds later, they heard a car door slam. Amanda sighed with relief, glad that it was finally over. After six years of living with the man, she could tell when he meant business. Jimmy wouldn't be back. That chapter was done.

Ryker stepped over to them, his eyes searching out her face. "Are you sure you're okay?" he asked her softly, uncaring of Jean's perusal.

"I'm fine," Amanda replied, wiping her palms down the front of her legs. Between Jimmy's threats and Ryker's heated gaze, she was sweating up a storm. "I'm just really glad that's over."

The sheriff spoke with them for several minutes before both men left. It was odd, Amanda hadn't realized that Ryker was so friendly with the other man. Luckily, the bar had remained empty the entire time. Otherwise the incident would have been all over Nashoba by nightfall.

"You're well rid of that one," Jean informed her, taking a sip from her coffee cup. She was back in her perch, the remote in her hand. "How you made it as long as you did, I'll never know."

Amanda didn't know either. He'd been her first boyfriend, though, and she'd felt loyalty to him. Jimmy hadn't deserved it. He hadn't deserved anything she'd given him, including her body. As much as she might want to, she couldn't change the past. She just had to accept it and move on, something she thought she was doing quite well.

Chapter 11

Amanda waited in the private room at Nashoba Memorial Hospital, the silence driving her crazy. She'd already read every magazine they'd had available, but none of them could hold her interest. She didn't understand the delay in starting her treatments, not that she was looking forward to them.

Upon her arrival, she'd immediately been taken for more tests. Ryker had accompanied her, but he never made it any further than the waiting room. Amanda actually preferred it that way. Something about him seeing her hooked up made her feel vulnerable in a way she couldn't really explain. She wanted him to see her as a healthy and desirable female, not the woman that the cancer had made her. A small part of her still secretly hoped that something could develop between them, but there would be no possibility if she kept rubbing her illness in his face.

She couldn't figure Ryker out. On one hand, he was the perfect man. He was kind, considerate, and he was always available, if she needed him. But there was nothing personal about his actions. His flirtations were gone. He treated her as if she were a valued friend, but nothing more. He certainly hadn't touched her again, and she hated it. Despite being sick, she still wanted him. There was nothing platonic about her feelings for Ryker.

The door opened, revealing her doctor. He smiled in greeting as he closed the door behind him.

Immediately, he started perusing the paperwork in his hand before staring at her. His expression turned grave.

"I'm sorry to keep you waiting so long," he informed her, moving to sit on one of the rolling stools beside her. "Normally I would have sent you home and had you to come into my office for the results, but I thought this might be too urgent to delay."

It felt as if an invisible band was tightening around her throat, but she forced herself to speak. "How bad is it?"

"It's bad," he said, without preamble. "The cancer is spreading, and your tumor has not shrunk. At this point, I don't feel as if additional treatments will help you. Do you understand what that means?"

Amanda gawked at him, her mind blank. It took a moment for his words to sink in. As much as she'd hoped for the better, it would appear it wasn't to be. She cleared her throat, praying that she wouldn't break down in front of him. "What you're saying is that I need to just enjoy the time I have left."

He nodded, the area around his mouth white. How many times had he had to give another patient the same news? Probably often. She felt bad for him. It couldn't be easy to tell person after person that their lives would soon be over. The doctor was just the messenger, though many people would probably not see it that way. Nobody wanted to know they were dying. Nobody.

"How long?" she whispered, looking down at

her clasped hands.

"Two months, maybe less," he replied, taking his glasses off to rub at his face with a napkin. "I'm very sorry to be the bearer of bad news. It's never easy, especially when it comes to someone as young as you are."

He fell silent, flipping through her chart. "The cancer has moved into your lungs, lymph nodes, and your liver," he continued. "And it's likely that it will continue to spread. It could possibly move into your brain. It wouldn't be uncommon. You've lost half of your body weight since starting the treatments. Some of it is from the cancer, but a lot of it is from the treatments. If we continued them, your side effects would only get worse, and I've seen enough to be able to tell you that they won't make a difference in your condition. They will only make you sicker than you need to be. If I thought for a moment they would help to prolong your life, I'd encourage you to continue. But I don't."

"What should I do?" she asked, her voice flat and lifeless.

"Enjoy what life you have left," he replied kindly. "When the disease progresses enough we have ways to keep you comfortable. At least this way you have a small window of time to live normally. It's been two weeks since your last chemo and radiation. Already it's clearing out of your system. Make each day matter and live it to the fullest."

Hot tears dripped down her face before falling

on her pants. As much as she hated to show it, she was devastated. "I'm scared," she admitted to him, her voice hoarse. "I don't know if I'm strong enough to face this. I'm afraid of dying."

"Do you have someone who can be with you?" he asked, his voice sympathetic. "It can make all the difference. This isn't a journey you need to undertake alone, Amanda."

Did she have someone? Would it even be fair to ask? Death wasn't just hard on the person who was dying, it was hard on the ones who were left behind, too. Maybe more so, because they had to go on living. Losing her parents had devastated her. And as she sat there facing her own death, she missed them even more. Could she really ask Ryker to care for her until the end? Amanda didn't know. She needed time to think on it.

He held out a card and a piece of paper. "I've gone ahead and set you up for an appointment at my office next week," he announced briskly, all business. "I've also wrote down the medicines I'd like you to continue taking, and the ones I'd like you to leave off. I want you to spend the next few days tying up your loose ends and figuring things out. If you're still feeling anxiety I can prescribe something for you next week, but I think you'll feel better once you have the future planned out."

"Thank you," she replied automatically, her thoughts sluggish. "Would it be all right if I took a few minutes alone before I left? I need some time to compose myself." She wasn't prepared to tell Ryker the truth. Not yet. He'd see right through her if she wandered out in her current condition.

"Take all the time you need," he reassured her, leaning over to pat her on the hand before standing up. "Make sure you don't forget your appointment. I'll expect to see you then."

He left, closing the door behind him with a gentle click. Amanda barely noticed his departure. Instead, she buried her face in her hands and sobbed like there was no tomorrow... and for her, that was a definite possibility.

* * * * *

Ryker ran a hand down his face, grimacing at the smell of the hospital. It wasn't that it had an obvious odor, at least it wouldn't for your average human, but for a werewolf it was terrible. The smell of death and debilitating illness nearly choked him. The odors originated from countless sources throughout the hospital, all of them contained within the walls of the building. Nausea churned in his gut. *God, I hate hospitals.*

"Are you all right, sir?" Ryker looked up to see an attractive woman next to him, her face concerned. In her hand she held a glace of ice water. *She must have been watching me like a hawk.* Ryker shook his head in a mixture of annoyance and disbelief. He could scent her interest in him, and he didn't like it. Didn't she realize it was a hospital, not a bar to pick up men?

"I'm fine, thank you," he said in a snappish voice, wishing she'd just leave him alone. There were several other people in the waiting room, he didn't see her attempting to ease their waits. "You might want to check with some of the others here," he informed her coldly. "I'm sure some of them would appreciate a kind word or something to drink."

Several of them overheard his words and nodded in approval. The waiting room was strictly for those with friends or family undergoing chemotherapy, and Ryker completely understood what they were going through. He'd never felt more helpless in his life. It was unbearable to watch someone you cared for wasting away, all the while knowing there was nothing you could do to stop it. His anguish was physical. He'd had a gnawing ache inside of him ever since discovering her condition.

I care for Amanda. Her future genuinely mattered to him, so much so it was scary. He'd never felt so protective toward a member of the opposite sex, or anyone for that matter, except for his parents. It had been so long ago that he'd nearly forgotten what it felt like.

In his musings, he'd all but forgotten the woman still standing next to him. She looked around the room with an expression of disdain on her carefully made up face before flipping her straightened hair over her shoulder. She was wearing scrubs, but Ryker didn't know if she was a nurse or a clerk. Either way, her bedside manner left a lot to be desired.

In the end, she ignored his last words, choosing to believe she still had a chance. "I'll be right over there," she drawled out, in a sugary sweet voice. "Let me know if you need anything, and I do mean *anything.*"

With that she turned and walked away, swinging her hips so wide that it would have been a danger to anyone that might have passed her by. *Ridiculous.*

The waiting room was surprisingly full of people. *So much pain and suffering.* It made Ryker yearn to be away from them, but strangely it made him yearn for the past, too. As old as he was, he'd been lucky enough to see several centuries.

With each new century the world had been amazed at the developments in communication and travel. There hadn't been any aspect of their lives that had remained untouched. Had it really been worth it, though? Nature was suffering, the ozone layer was nearly destroyed, and the quality of the air they breathed was not very good. No longer could people drink from the rivers and streams—the very water created to sustain them. They were too polluted and filled with chemicals to be safe.

Animals still drank from them, though, at least those that were able to survive the overpopulation of the world, and the ridiculous number of cars constantly on the roads. In their innocence, they didn't realize that the world was no longer safe for them. There was no place for them now, not anymore.

He missed the days when people had peace in their lives, a time when animals and people lived freely. It was nearly impossible now, not with all of the pressures and responsibilities they had. How long could humanity continue at the pace they had set for themselves? Their advances and technology had come at staggering prices, not only financially but in their personal lives as well.

One thing that hadn't changed with the centuries was the greed and need for control. There had always been power struggles, and there always would be. It was the way people worked. No matter how many might crave peace, there would always be someone determined to control them. It happened to both human and werewolf alike, proven by Alexander's current situation.

Soon he would have to leave to accompany his king to Australia. He hated to leave Amanda, but he had no choice. Despite his reluctance, his wolf was eager to engage and destroy the threat. There would be no peace in their lives until the challenge was completed, but he felt confident about their success. They were just *that* good.

Ryker scented her seconds before he saw her, her scent a refreshing change from those that surrounded him. To his surprise, she was still mostly free from the toxins that contaminated her after each treatment. Coming to his feet, he met her as she started across the room. "What's happened?" Ryker asked immediately, looking past her to the door that she'd come from. Although she was composed, he could just *feel* that something was wrong. Very wrong.

"Nothing," Amanda replied, her voice calm. "Let's get out of here."

She turned without another word, heading for the exit. Ryker followed her, frowning. "Did your treatments go pretty well for you today?" he asked her, fishing for information. "You don't seem as weak as you usually are."

Amanda just shrugged, her face averted from his. "Physically, I don't feel as bad as I usually do," she replied, noncommittally. "So I can't complain about that."

Once they were outside in the parking lot, Amanda surprised him by grabbing his arm to stop him. "I'm thinking about going away for the next few days. Would it be all right with you if I did? I'm already off from the bar." She looked past him, her blue eyes appearing to be in some faraway place. "I need a break from all of this; you know what I mean?"

In the sun, her golden hair appeared to glow. She was beautiful to him, ethereal even, with her dreamy eyes and pale face. For a moment, he had difficulty even processing her words. He was positive he'd never seen a more beautiful sight in his life.

"I'll take you wherever you'd like to go," he volunteered, willing to promise her anything. Why hadn't he thought of it before? "I could use a break myself. Where would you like to go? The world is literally at your disposal. London? Egypt? A tropical island? I own a few places internationally, and what I don't own I've got connections." He grinned at her, enjoying her bemused expression.

She watched him carefully, warily even, as if she didn't fully believe his offer. Who could blame her, though? It wasn't as if many men in rural Missouri could or would be able to take her on such a grand trip, especially on such a short notice. He wasn't most men, though, and his offer wasn't entirely unselfish. He wanted to take her away somewhere exotic, somewhere seductive. Remaining abstinent in her presence was killing him, slowly and painfully, especially with her natural scent clearly returning.

"What about your job?" Her eyes searched his face, her expression filled with hope. "Wouldn't you get fired?"

Ryker laughed. "Not a chance," he reassured her. *If she only knew.* "And believe me, I'm overdue for a lot of vacation time."

"I couldn't be gone for long," Amanda told him, frowning as she appeared to consider it. "I would have to be back by Monday so I can do Jean's books. I hate leaving it for so long, but I don't think she'd mind if I took off Friday." Ryker knew the other woman had already given her a few days off for her treatments, and she didn't want Amanda doing the books on the weekends.

"Would that work okay for you?" she asked hesitantly. "I hate to impose on you any further, especially considering all that you have done for me already. Really, I don't mind going away by myself. I just need to clear my head."

Amanda broke off to look away but not before Ryker saw the brief flash of hurt in her eyes. After a small pause, she added, "You've been really distant lately. I don't want you to take me just because you feel bad for me. If you're doing this because you would genuinely like to get away, I'm okay with that. But if you're just doing this out of compassion, I'd rather be alone."

He started to speak, but she held up a hand to stop him. "You don't want a relationship with me, and I get this. I wasn't born yesterday. Obviously you feel as if a mistake was made, but you don't have to worry that I can't accept you don't want to be with me. I can. I have. Getting involved with someone that has cancer is kind of a lose-lose situation, huh?" she smiled grimly.

"But I don't want things to be tense and miserable between us. I can't take any more of it. I feel like I'm walking around on pins and needles. I can accept just being friends. Can you? Because if you can't, I need to know now. Just say the word, and I'll move out today. Either way, all of this uncomfortableness stops now."

Hell, no, I can't accept that. A platonic friendship was way too mild a term for what he craved with her. How could she even think that? The sex between them had been hotter than anything he'd ever experienced before. Ryker fantasized day and night about finding his way back into her bed... and between her legs. But how the hell was he supposed to seduce her, when he was terrified his seduction would harm her?

He was fucked up, but even worse, he didn't have any answers. He'd never been so unsure of himself, and it was messing with him. If he didn't say something, though, she would be gone. Of that he was certain. "I have to admit I've had a lot on my mind," he finally confessed, gently leading her to his SUV. "There's a lot going on at work, and I'm having to devote a lot of time and energy to that. This trip is going to be good for both of us, so let's not over think it. The last thing I want if for you to move out."

He winced, but Amanda didn't see it. As far as answers went, it had to be the shittiest one in existence. Until he worked it out in his own mind, though, it wouldn't be fair to either one of them for him to say anything else. All he knew was that he wanted her, badly, and if the erection in his pants had any say in it, he would be having her again. *Soon.*

Chapter 12

Amanda took a sip from her glass, enjoying the taste of the fine wine on her tongue. For the first time in a long time, she felt peaceful. Relaxed. Earlier that evening Ryker had gone fishing, returning with a huge catch. He'd even gone so far as to fillet and cook them. It was just one of several relaxing meals they'd shared since arriving on the island.

"I could have given you London or France," Ryker mused from across the table, his face warm and relaxed. "But you picked an island in Alaska. I can't really complain, though. I've always enjoyed coming up here." He'd informed her upon their arrival that he owned the island.

"How have you stayed away so long?" she asked him, once again admiring the glossy woodwork. The house was huge, with every amenity known to man. It wasn't just the house that drew her to the island, though. It was the island itself; it was a magical place.

Since arriving, they'd fished, boated, and walked across the shoreline too many times to count. The weather was a little chilly at times but not so bad she couldn't enjoy it comfortably. In Alaska, it was easy to forget all of her problems, especially since she was feeling so much better. The treatments had really made her sick. If nothing else, at least she wouldn't have to suffer through those again.

Ryker shrugged, the motion pulling her eyes to

his broad chest and shoulders. The golden glow from the muted lights did wonderful things to his skin. He was attractive enough to take her breath away, but the feeling didn't appear to be mutual. Everything had been strictly platonic since their arrival. Ryker was cheerful and friendly, but that was it. A twinge of pain and regret shot through her chest. She'd foolishly hoped for more.

"Surprisingly enough, it wasn't that hard," he admitted, giving her a wry grin. "It's easy to get tied up in day-to-day life, isn't it? Somewhere down the line, my job became my life. Besides, I've already traveled extensively, and after a while it just gets old."

"Maybe so, but still," she replied, "I couldn't have made it as long as you have. Not when I knew I had a place like this to come to. It's been wonderful. Thanks for bringing me."

Their idyllic getaway would be over soon. They were returning to Missouri the day following the next, and it would be back to reality for Amanda. This was her final trip. The thought made her sad.

"Nonsense," Ryker replied, coming to his feet. "You make the perfect traveling companion. Where have you been all my life?" he teased her, coming around the table to pull her chair back. "I cringe when I think of all the missed adventures we could have had."

Grabbing her hands, he pulled her to her feet. For a moment they just stood there, their bodies only inches apart. He stared into her face with the eyes of a lover, hot and heated. *Would he kiss her?* Her lips parted as she held her breath, unable to look away.

"Come with me," Ryker muttered hoarsely, as if he too were caught up in the spell of the moment. He turned away, but not before Amanda missed the look of regret on his face. She didn't understand his reluctance to kiss her, but he felt the same attraction she did. She'd seen it. "There's something I want to show you."

She followed him out on the deck, breathing deeply of the refreshing coolness of the air. Ryker had an amazing deck, one that extended completely across the front of the house. Set up high on beams, they had an amazing view of the ocean and shoreline.

The sun was about to set. "See over there," he said, pointing at the shoreline. "This is nature at its finest."

Amanda turned her face to look, immediately gasping with pleasure. A momma bear stood in the water, with three cubs frolicking in the rocks behind her. From the size of them, they couldn't have been very old. The mother bear was looking for their evening meal. She wasn't having much luck.

"They are beautiful," Amanda whispered, charmed by the touching scene in front of her. Every so often she would turn around to check on her babies, but her focus was on the hunt. Eventually, one of the babies wandered into the water, but it didn't go far. It quickly lost interest, returning back to its brothers and sisters to play.

"You're right," she told Ryker, wiping at her teary eyes with her hand. "This really is nature at its finest. Here on your island the bears feel safe, and it's awe-inspiring to see them so free. It's so sad to think that one day they might be hunted or killed."

"Not here," Ryker denied vehemently. His dark eyebrows pulled together as his hands clenched the railing. "I don't allow any hunting on this island. *Ever*, not even during hunting season. I can't protect the whole state of Alaska, but I can make the rules for my own property. I don't believe in hunting for sport, and I won't tolerate it on my land."

She hadn't realized he felt so strongly about it, but it relieved her. The bears would have a long and peaceful life. One day they would grow up and have cubs of their own, and their life cycle would continue. It was a beautiful thought.

"You know, I think I could stay here forever," she told him, enchanted by the moment. "Here on the island, it's almost like time stands still. There's no pressure, no responsibilities. If there really was a Heaven on earth, it would have to be here. This is paradise."

Ryker took the glass from her hand, setting it on the wooden ledge. He turned her to face him, slowly sliding his hands around her waist. Amanda trembled, his touch setting her on fire. It was the moment she'd been waiting for.

His eyes were serious as he watched her reaction, his movements unhurried. "Staying here wouldn't be a hardship," he told her in a deep voice. "If I knew you'd be here, too." His head lowered, his mouth slowly moving closer to hers.

"There's no place I'd rather be," she whispered, just an instant before he took her lips. Ryker kissed her gently, taking his sweet time. Eventually, she felt the press of his tongue against the seam of her lips. And that quickly, everything changed.

The need that existed within both of them could no longer be denied. "Take me upstairs," she groaned against his lips. He growled at her words, lifting her straight up into his arms. Carrying her through the house, he took her upstairs and into his bedroom before setting her down on her feet. But he didn't release her. Instead he kissed his way over to her ear as he said, "I want to make love to you, Amanda. Badly. If you want me to stop, tell me now."

"I don't want to stop," she moaned back, enjoying the sensations his firm lips created within her. Her hands slid down to his waistband as she tugged at his shirt. Pulling it free from his pants she slid her hands underneath, groaning at the feel of his skin.

She wanted him as much as he did her, maybe even more. She needed him. Being with Ryker restored the part of her that felt undesirable and unloved. Everyone she was around treated her with pity... like a woman that was in the last stages of her life. And though she might be, with Ryker she didn't feel that way. In his arms, she felt passionate and alive.

"I want to pleasure you," she told him, her

hands moving to unbutton his shirt. It was a bold statement, something she would have never said to Jimmy. She hadn't desired him like she did Ryker, though.

Sliding the shirt from his shoulders, she leaned forward to kiss his chest. Ryker groaned loudly, his own hands sliding up to cup her breasts. "God, yes," he replied, emphatically. "Do whatever you want with me. I'm yours for the taking."

Amanda had to smile at the raw passion behind his words. Knowing that he wanted her increased her own daring... and her arousal.

She finished undressing him while he watched her, his blue eyes ablaze with passion. "Touch me," he encouraged her, his voice soft. His large cock was erect and fully extended, his head brushing against her. "I want to feel your hands on me."

He pulled her face to his, kissing her until she was dizzy. Heat built up within her, her desire pooling in the area deep between her legs. Both of her hands explored his shaft, emboldened by the deep groan that vibrated from deep within his body.

His weight in her hands felt so right. Her thumb brushed across the slit in his crown, teasing it in circles when she felt the wetness of his arousal. For the first time in her life, she was tempted to taste it. And as soon as the thought popped up in her mind, she was powerless to stop it.

Shakily, she lowered herself to her knees before staring up at him, a wordless plea on her face.

Ryker made a noise in the back of his throat, his hands sliding forward to brush her hair back from her face. She could feel the trembling in his large, gentle hands, and in that moment she lost her fear. He knew what she wanted to do, and God help her he *approved*.

"I've never done this before," she whispered, tentatively grasping his thick length. Could she even fit her lips around such a wide width? She was determined to find out.

"Good," Ryker told her, his voice thick with his sexy accent. He adjusted his stance until his feet were further apart, his cock jutting out proudly.

"What if I hurt you?" Amanda's mouth all but watered. She was hungry for the taste of him. The thought of giving him pleasure in that manner nearly made her orgasm herself.

"*Hurt me*," he groaned out, his eyes shutting in pleasure. He acted as if the thought aroused him beyond belief. "As long as your mouth is on me, I couldn't care less."

His words empowered her. Using one hand to hold him in place, she decided to start with the head and work her way down. Drawing him to her lips, her tongue snaked out to taste him as she shuddered in delight.

* * * * *

The pleasure was incredible. Ryker was so turned on that he thought he might blow at any moment. Amanda wasn't the first female to pleasure him in such a way, but none of his past experiences could began to compare to what he felt as her tongue worked him so eagerly. And heaven help him, she hadn't even taken him fully into her hot little mouth yet.

He couldn't deny his masculine pride at knowing she'd never suckled another man's cock. Sex was intimate, but so was her oral pleasuring. He vowed that he would be the only man she ever did this to. Ever. For his decision was clear. Upon his return from the challenge, he was changing Amanda. No longer did it matter to him that she wasn't his mate. What he felt for her was too strong to ignore, and he couldn't, wouldn't, live without her.

Ryker murmured words of encouragement, his head thrown back as he fought to hold onto his control. He was so lost to the pleasure that he wasn't even sure what he was saying. Her heated mouth slipped over his crown as he groaned in delight. His shaft filled her mouth completely. The tight seal sent him into a vortex of pleasure so great he feared he'd turn.

"I can't hold it back," Ryker warned her, expecting her to release him immediately. She didn't. If anything his words seemed to send her into a frenzy. One of her hands slid down to his balls, cupping them as she suckled him even deeper.

"Sweetheart, if you don't stop I'm going to fill that delectable mouth full," he warned her again. His balls were tight and heat was spiraling up his shaft. It was just a matter of seconds.

Amanda groaned around him, her eyes opening

to stare into his. They were dazed with passion—heated and lusty. She wrapped her other hand around the base of his shaft, squeezing him with just the right amount of pressure as it kept time with her mouth. *Heaven help me, she is milking me for my seed,* Ryker realized, his hands unconsciously guiding her head in an effort to help her fulfill her mission. *Well, by God, she is going to get it.*

Ryker exploded, breathing harshly as his release spurted out of him and into her greedy little mouth. His orgasm was earth shattering, so much so his vision briefly blurred. Instead of being satisfied, though, an unholy arousal shot through him. Ryker felt animalistic, his wolf rising to the forefront as if he wanted to claim her. As puzzling as it was, he was too far gone to control it. There was only one cure for the problem that ailed him, and it rested in the tight area between her legs.

Amanda released his fully erect cock with a distinct pop, her eyes dreamy with arousal. He pulled her to her feet, undressing her with a desperation that surprised him. He wanted her naked and spread out for his pleasure—for his penetration. He had to be inside.

"That was just the beginning," Ryker promised her, making a small sound of appreciation when he bared her breasts. He couldn't resist leaning over to suckle each one, enjoying the taste and sensation. "Your breasts are so beautiful," he growled, forcing his face away to continue on his journey. He couldn't linger. He wanted her too badly to delay.

He could scent her arousal through her jeans, and it maddened him. Amanda remained still, but there was no denying how much she wanted him. It was there in the heat of her eyes, the scent from her body, and the tight little buds on her chest. She wouldn't have complained if he'd ripped her jeans off and plunged in, in fact, he was willing to bet she craved it. The knowledge almost undid him.

His fingers dipped between her legs, trailing along the seam of her jeans. Her arousal was so strong that wetness saturated the material. His cock jerked in pleasure, needing to penetrate her tight folds. He wanted to put her on all fours, pumping into her until he could pump no more.

Somehow, he regained control. Thoughts of her illness penetrated his hazy mind. He couldn't take her as he'd like, but that didn't mean he couldn't have her. Working her jeans down her thighs, he murmured, "Now, it's my turn. Let me know if the pleasure gets to be too much."

* * * * *

Amanda shivered at his words, her body a bottomless pit of desire. She enjoyed suckling him more than she'd ever dreamed. Tasting his seed had been the hottest, most decadent thing she'd ever done. She wanted to do it again. Soon.

"Bring it on," she taunted him daringly. "I'd like to see what you have to bring to the table."

Finished with her jeans, he met her eyes. "Would you now? All I can say is you'd better be very hungry," he finished with a growl, backing her up to the bed. "Because I'm expecting you to gorge yourself on it. I'd hate for there to be any leftovers," he continued, watching as she climbed in. "Especially since it's a special preparation."

"What do you mean?" Amanda murmured, aroused beyond belief by their bantering and foreplay.

"This," he replied simply, burying his face between her legs. His fingers parted her lips, his tongue tasting her deeply. "Mmm," he growled. "This is the best appetizer I've ever had."

"Maybe you should try it again," she suggested breathlessly, her hips arching in invitation. "Just to make sure."

He did, and Amanda forgot to think. Her body tightened nearly immediately as she spiraled toward an orgasm.

Ryker slid a finger deep within. Then to her surprise, she felt another finger further down. He gently wet it in her juices before rubbing his thumb in circles across her puckered skin. With his tongue hammering at her nub, she was mindless with pleasure.

Amanda had never been touched there before. After a brief moment of hesitation, she went with it. The sensation of two fingers at both entries was erotic enough to convince her to let him play. Beyond that, though, she trusted him to know what he was doing. He was the best she'd ever had in bed. The man was an amazing lover.

His tongue swept repeatedly across her clit. She groaned, hovering at the very edge of her orgasm. At the same time, Ryker slid his thumb into virgin territory. The sensation of being so full was her undoing.

"Ryker," she screamed, riding his thumb, face, and finger. Her entire world exploded in front of her eyes, and she was drowning in the pleasure. "Oh, my God," she sobbed out, uncontrollably. Her orgasm went on and on.

Letting his fingers slide away, Ryker lifted his body up from between her legs. Leaning over her chest, he started to kiss and play with her breasts. Without any warning he rolled over, pulling her down on top of him. He immediately resumed his actions, his fingers teasing her breasts with a skill that left her wanting more.

Her nether lips rested over his shaft. The temptation was too strong to resist, especially with his mouth working her breasts so well. "I'm not full yet," she told him, her voice shaky with desire.

Ryker broke off long enough to grin at her, his sexy face full of promise. "You will be," he said. "I can guarantee you that."

Reaching down between their bodies, he guided his shaft into position. "Ride me, Amanda," he muttered seductively. "I want to feel that heated pussy while I suckle on these big breasts."

He didn't have to ask twice. Instinct took over, showing her what she needed to know. Ryker guided her hips, but only for a moment. The pleasure of her movements soon possessed her as she moved in an age old rhythm that needed no instruction.

Chapter 13

"Good morning, sexy," Ryker drawled out, close to her ear. His front was pressed against her back, his arm wrapped around her as his hand cupped her breast. His turgid erection was pressed into her back. The man was insatiable.

She mock groaned at his words, turning to burrow her face into the pillow. "I feel like I've only slept for a few minutes," she complained, but she couldn't help grinning. She felt great, despite the soreness of her body. They'd made love nearly all night, only stopping once the sun had risen. On this island, she'd well and truly found paradise. If she didn't know better, she'd think it was a dream.

Ryker chuckled. "I guess I'll have to keep you in bed all day," he informed her, his fingers moving on her nipple. "Although I can't promise that you'll be sleeping."

Amanda didn't immediately reply. God, it was tempting, but the soreness within her was pretty strong. She wasn't sure if her body was capable of taking him again so soon, but how could she tell him that? She was worried he'd take it as a sign of rejection.

As if he'd read her mind, he continued, "But first I need to feed you."

"That sounds good," she replied automatically, her thoughts heavy. There was something more important that she needed to share, and it had nothing to do with her soreness. Before things progressed any further, she had to come clean with him. He had a right to know about her decision, even if the thought of confessing left a bitter taste in her mouth.

With one last nuzzle at her neck, he rolled over to come to his feet. Her next words stopped him. "I've stopped my cancer treatments."

Ryker grabbed her shoulder, gently turning her over in the bed to face him. He stared down at her in disbelief. "I don't get it. What do you mean you stopped your treatments? Why on earth would you want to?" He looked genuinely puzzled.

She caught her lower lip with her teeth, gently pressing down. Having this conversation with him was hard. How was she supposed to tell him that the woman he'd just slept with was dying? As far as pillow chat went, it was pretty morbid.

But she couldn't ignore his questions. "I didn't have any treatments the other day," she explained, wishing she could get out of the bed. Unfortunately she was naked, though, so she had no choice but to remain. As close as they were, her every emotion was revealed. It made her nervous. "But I've got an appointment with the doctor this upcoming week."

Ryker stared at her incredulously. "That's it?" he said somewhat sarcastically, coming to his feet. He kept his back to her, as if he'd grown tired of looking at her. Who knew? Maybe he had. "You've already established that you're no longer doing the treatments. What I want to know is why."

His words angered her. "You know, I'm really tired of being questioned," she told him, wrapping the sheet around her body. Coming to her own feet, she stalked away from the bed, heading in the opposite direction. She wanted her clothes, she felt ridiculous having their conversation naked. "In fact, I'm just about tired of everything. I'm tired of people treating me as if I'm just a doormat, you know, someone to wipe their feet on anytime they pass through. I've had to deal with it from everyone, except for a select few, and it has gotten old. It seems like no matter what I do, I just can't ever seem to win."

She picked out some clothing before turning back to stare at him. "And now I have you questioning everything I do as if I don't have the wisdom to make the right choices for my own body. Don't you think I have my best interests at heart? My God, you act as if I need to run my treatment choices by you first, just to get your approval."

Amanda stopped, struggling for control. Ryker had overstepped his boundaries, but still her problems weren't due to him. Mostly. And with that in mind, she continued, "Look, I appreciate everything you've done, and I hope that you know that. But just because you've done these things doesn't mean I owe you any explanations. We're not even in a relationship. As far as I can tell the only thing between us is sex, and we both know that means little more than nothing." It hurt, but it was the truth. Ryker had mentioned nothing about commitment. The sex was fantastic, but even that didn't take the sting away.

And at that moment, his cell phone rang.

* * * * *

Ryker stared at Amanda, his hands on his hips as he ignored his phone. He was completely frustrated. If he were completely honest with himself, though, he couldn't blame her for her reaction. He had enjoyed her body without ever giving any indication that it meant more than that. But how could it have gone any differently? He was just coming to terms with his feelings himself.

Expelling a heavy rush of air, he grabbed his phone off the table. "I have to take this," he muttered, looking down at the caller id. It was Alexander's personal number, which meant it was extremely important. "I'm not done with this conversation, though," he warned her, an instant before answering.

"Ryker," he answered in a clipped tone, his eyes following her as she left the room. With one last glare over her shoulder she shut the bathroom door, her arms full of clothing.

"It's Alexander," the other man told him. There was a pause of silence that spoke in volumes before he continued, "I'm going to get straight to the point. I need you to come back."

"The date is set?" Ryker asked him, although he already knew the answer.

"We leave out tomorrow morning. Early," Alexander confirmed, his voice as cold as ice. "I don't need to tell you to return as soon as possible. We'll be flying out well before dawn, and we still have a lot to do. Are you own affairs in order?"

Ryker knew what he was asking. He wanted to know if he'd made arrangements, should he not return. Although he felt rather unconcerned about the challenge, he did realize how serious it was. There were no guarantees. Their opponents were well-trained, vicious werewolf fighters.

"Of course," he told Alexander. "I made a will a long time ago, although it does have to be updated throughout the years."

What he didn't tell Alexander was that he'd changed it the week before. Should something happen to him, the majority of his wealth would be handed over to Amanda. Why not? It wasn't as if he had any family to leave it to, and he couldn't think of anyone more deserving of it than she was. And though he felt confident he'd return, what if he didn't? The thought of leaving her penniless and alone to fend for herself was inconceivable. What he hadn't left to her, he'd left to cancer charities. Her illness had affected him deeply.

"Very good," Alexander replied, his voice filled with approval. It was the first time during the call that he'd actually relaxed. Back at Wolf Town, stress levels had to be through the roof. "Should we expect you tonight?"

"At the latest." He wouldn't have time to make things right with Amanda, more the pity. He would when he returned, though. He vowed it. "I'm going to call the airline now, it's still early enough that I shouldn't have any problems. I'll call back with an update, once I find out which flight we'll be on." It would probably cost him an arm and a leg to find a same-day flight, but it couldn't be helped.

The two men hung up as Amanda walked out. Her face was pale, but she was composed. "We are going to have to leave early," Ryker informed her, moving to the closet to select his own clothing. He was still naked, but it didn't bother him. He was completely comfortable nude.

"How early," Amanda asked him, moving closer. A flicker of hurt crossed her face, but she concealed it quickly. "Does this have something to do with me?"

"No!" He stopped to look at her, shaking his head in denial. "That was my boss on the phone, and he needs me back as soon as possible. Do you remember me telling you that I would have to be gone for awhile?" He waited for her to nod before continuing, "That time is now. We're leaving out early in the morning, which doesn't leave us much time. Unless you'd like to remain here?" It wasn't a bad idea.

She went to get her own bag before placing it on the bed. It took her a moment to answer, as if she were considering it. "I don't think that would be a good idea, at least not by myself. Besides, I can't miss my appointment."

Her appointment. There was so much unfinished business between them. The challenge couldn't have come at a worst time, but then again

Ryker was relieved that it would be finished. He was a werewolf, and they never backed down. Ever. They hadn't been the ones to start it, but they'd certainly be the ones to finish it. It was going to be one hell of a fight, in actuality a bloodbath. His wolf was practically jumping for joy. Once he got back, Amanda would be the center of his attention. She'd have to be. He was going to turn her.

Already dressed, Ryker finished packing his stuff, a task that was performed in only a matter of minutes. As a guardian he was used to traveling light. There was still a lot left to do, though. He had several phone calls to make, including one to the caretaker and housekeeper. Luckily for him, they were married. They lived on the island and took care of it year-round. As far as his home went, he was leaving it in good hands.

Ryker walked over to Amanda, turning her away from her packing. She stared up at him in surprise, her eyes wary as if she wasn't sure what to expect from him next. Underneath the supernatural strength of his hands, her frame felt so small and fragile. She'd lost a considerable amount of weight since he'd met her, a fact that he hated. Not only did it worry him, but he actually preferred her at a Rubenesque size. Her weight loss was a visible reminder of her illness and how quickly it was ravaging her body.

"You and I, we've got a lot to talk about," he told her softly, his eyes memorizing every inch of her face. No matter what size she was, Amanda would always be beautiful to him. "What I have to say to you can't be said in a matter of moments, though, which is why I want to ask you to please wait for me. I don't want you moving out or making any spur-of-the-moment decisions about your future while I'm gone. I promise you I'll explain when I get back, if you'll promise me that you'll wait."

His words appeared to soften her. She looked down and nodded, her blonde wig firmly on her head. She'd slept in it the night before, but Ryker wouldn't have minded if she hadn't. She still wasn't comfortable enough to go without it in front of him. He planned on changing that fact when he came back.

He couldn't explain why he felt so strongly about her, and he was fine with that. All he knew was that he couldn't let her go. Did she feel the same way? It might have been wishful thinking, but he believed she did. Clearly, she enjoyed his body. It was enough for him, at least for the moment.

"I won't leave," she promised him, her voice little more than a whisper. "I owe you at least that much."

"Good," he replied, in a teasing voice. "Will you look at me now?"

She raised her head, a light sheen of tears in her eyes. "Wherever you're going, will you be safe? Somehow this just doesn't feel like the average business trip."

Amanda was intuitive, far more than he would

have guessed. She'd also asked the one question he couldn't answer. So he did what any normal, red-blooded male would have done. He kissed her deeply, hoping that his passionate embrace would be enough to distract her from her question.

It worked, but Ryker hadn't counted on the backlash. At the first taste of her honeyed lips, he was lost as well. In the end, it was a long time before the two of them left his island... or his room.

* * * * *

Upon his arrival, Wolf Town was ablaze with activity. Although the hour was late, it didn't matter to the werewolves. Every citizen was up, or so it seemed. The street was filled with wolves and guardians rushing to and from, most of them with their hands filled with... something. Although the majority of them would remain in Missouri, it didn't stop them from contributing. Pack supported pack, no matter what the need was. It was just their way.

Ryker strolled into headquarters as if he owned it, a satisfied grin on his face. Despite the gravity of the situation, he'd never felt better. Circumstances had forced him to leave a lot unsaid when it came to Amanda, but at least he had the reassurance that she'd be waiting for him when he came back. For the first time in his life, he nearly felt complete.

Connor and Orlando were standing in the main lobby by the elevators. Both men appeared disgruntled. They were attempting to organize what looked to be hundreds of duffel bags. Or at least

Orlando was. Connor stood with his arms crossed and a disdainful expression on his face as he bossed the other guardian around.

"Put all of them up against the wall," he told Orlando, who had already bent over and was tossing them with a speed that the average human couldn't have matched. "Why in the hell are they here anyhow? Wouldn't it have made more sense for the other guardians to drop their gear off at the air strip?"

Orlando just shrugged. He was quite a bit younger than the majority of the guardians, but Ryker liked him. He just didn't understand him. Orlando's choice of cars and music were atrocious, as was his ever-changing hair colors. It wasn't uncommon to see the other man with purple or green hair; he dyed it like some guardians changed clothing.

The younger guardian had settled down quite a bit, ever since the loss of his Pinto. Ryker shuddered. He hated thinking about the small car, especially since the night he got stuck in it. With its constant backfiring and shitty sound system, the Pinto had been obnoxiously loud. Everyone at Wolf Town had hated the car, and its days had been numbered.

Unfortunately for Orlando, a tree had somehow fallen on it. Or maybe the tree got a little help, or so Ryker suspected. Fate had presented the guardians with the perfect opportunity to permanently put the Pinto out of commission, and Ryker was willing to bet that one of them had been smart enough to realize it. The last time Ryker had seen it, the car had resembled a pancake. *Rest in peace.*

"And what the hell are in these bags?" Connor continued, his voice puzzled. "Damn, you'd think we're escorting a group of beauty pageant contestants or something. These idiots pack even more than women do. I mean, really. How much can a man need? We're only going to be gone for a few days."

Orlando tossed the last bag against the wall before straightening up with a groan. Ryker wasn't sure if the groan was due to exertion or Connor's bitching. "Oh, hey, Ryker," Orlando said, his face lighting up in greeting. If nothing else, he was always friendly. "Long time no see, man."

Ryker nodded stiffly. He knew he came off as a hard ass to the other guardians, but he'd never felt quite comfortable with them. He was serious by nature, while the majority of the others were always goofing off. Often their jokes and pranks crossed the line, and a good deal of them were generally directed towards him. It was amazing that they'd managed to work together for so many years without someone dying.

Connor turned his head to stare at him with a raised eyebrow, slowly perusing his face. To Ryker's surprise, though, he actually remained quiet. It was a welcome change from Connor's usual snarky comments.

"Alexander is over at the air field," Orlando continued, stopping to take a drink from a water bottle. "He's going over the flight plans. He said to tell you that he'll meet you here when he's done."

Ryker nodded before walking over to place his bag on top of the others. Despite the activity outside of headquarters, the interior was reasonably quiet. He turned back to face Connor and Orlando. "What part of Australia are we headed to?"

"The western side," Connor answered him, walking over to a chair to sprawl in it. "Ironically enough, the challenge is going to be held at the Wolf Creek Crater." He rolled his eyes as he said it. Clearly, Connor wasn't too impressed with the location.

To Ryker, though, it actually made perfect sense. The crater was located in a very remote area known as the Kimberley region. Combined with the ridge, the crater was nature's version of a stadium, and there would be more than enough room for the challenge to take place. It was unlikely they'd be disturbed by humans, but Ryker was sure that precautions would be in place to prevent anyone from entering. Just in case.

"The biggest disadvantage is the crater itself," Ryker mused out loud. "At least to us. On the ridge, the Australian pack can fully surround us. I don't trust them, especially once it's clear we will leave victoriously." And he hated tight, enclosed spaces, which was why he'd disliked Orlando's Pinto so much. "There are a lot of things that could go wrong."

Connor looked serious. "That's what I thought, too. We're taking a lot more guardians than originally planned, which means we're taking more planes. We won't be arriving at the exact same times, though. We wouldn't want to make ourselves too predictable for our Australian mates, now would we?"

"What about here, though? We can't leave Wolf Town vulnerable, especially after all the attacks we've experienced lately." It seemed like every time some of their guardians were gone, something unpleasant happened.

Connor groaned at his words, running his hand over the stubble on his face. He actually looked tired, something Ryker wasn't used to seeing from the other man. Then again, he'd recently spent a great deal of time injured. Truth be told, Connor was lucky to be alive. He'd sustained some serious injuries, even for a werewolf.

"And that is the whole crux of the problem, isn't it?" Connor muttered, as if he were speaking to himself. "You know, a year ago I wouldn't have been concerned over something like that, but a lot has changed since then. I'm mated, and we all know that Natalie is expecting. In fact, we've got quite a few mated wolves now, and leaving them behind to go across the world isn't easy. I couldn't take it if something happened, and I wasn't here to protect Natalie. When you mate, it really does change all the rules, huh? Natalie means more to me than anything. Life wouldn't be worth living, not if I lost her."

Ryker was surprised at his words, but he was careful to conceal it from the other man. He was seeing a side of Connor he'd never seen before, and he respected it. Even more, he emphasized with him. His feelings for Amanda were very similar, and he was glad she wouldn't be staying there in Wolf Town. Changing her before he left would have put her in danger. As it was she would be safe in his home, without any ties to the werewolf community. It was dangerous times for them, it would have been even worse for a woman trying to adjust to her new life as a supernatural creature.

"Dudes, chill," Orlando told them, staring at each man as if they'd just sprouted extra heads. "Everything is going to be fine. Alexander has got it all covered. Don't you remember? With the other packs pitching in, there are going to be a ton of werewolves here. Plus, he's leaving Ivan in charge. Do you really think he'd leave Carole Anne behind if he thought she was in danger?"

Hell, no. The king would turn down the challenge before he'd ever put his mate and unborn child at risk. Wolf Town had been taught several hard lessons over the prior year, and they had all learned from them. It was likely their settlement would be filled to the point of bursting with loyal werewolves who would defend their queen to the death. Alexander wouldn't settle for less.

Connor leaned forward, his eyes narrowed in speculation as he sniffed the air. Ryker stared back at him, his lips tightening in annoyance. "You got a problem, Bouchard?" If he did, he was messing with the wrong werewolf. Ryker wouldn't think twice about kicking his ass. It would just be a warm up for the upcoming match.

The other man looked thoughtful, which instantly put Ryker on alert. It was scary when Connor decided to actually use his brain. There was no telling what he'd come up with.

"I don't have a problem, *Connell*," Connor retorted pointedly, settling back into his chair. "I thought for a moment that you might, though." His eyes slid over to Orlando. "And unfortunately you too, considering you're the only other person in the room."

Orlando and Ryker exchanged uneasy looks. "What the fuck are you talking about?" Ryker hissed, staring angrily at Connor. "I have to warn you, I'm really not in the mood for your shit tonight."

Connor looked bored at his words. "For a moment, you smelled *mated*."

"Oh, hell, no," Orlando exclaimed, flushing uncomfortably. "Dude, that's so uncool."

"It was a logical conclusion," Connor replied as he shrugged. "But look on the bright side. Even if Ryker had mated you, you didn't mate him."

Ryker flexed his hands. He all but trembled with the need to wrap them around Connor's throat and squeeze. *Tightly*. "That has got to be the stupidest thing I've ever heard," he growled at him. "Do you spend your off time dreaming up this shit, or does this kind of stupidity just come naturally?"

Connor looked away as if he were checking for someone's arrival, but not before Ryker saw the satisfied grin on his face. "Oh, well," Connor murmured smoothly. "At least the two of you won't have to spend the rest of your nearly immortal lives spooning each other every night."

Alexander walked through the front door with Ivan, followed by several guardians. He took one look at their faces and immediately sized up the situation. "Connor," he said briskly, in a voice that left no doubt as to who was in charge. "Go get one of the jeeps. I want you to load it up with these bags and get them over to the planes. Now."

"With Orlando?" he asked hopefully, coming to his feet. Orlando sighed heavily. It was easy to see he dreaded going with Connor. How many hours had he already been stuck with him, putting up with his bossy ways? Orlando was too nice. Ryker would have already told him to fuck off.

"By yourself," Alexander bit out, rolling his eyes in exasperation. "Put on your big girl panties and get busy. There have been some changes in the departure schedules, and our flights have been moved up. The first plane leaves within the hour, and we're going to be on it. We have no time to waste."

Connor nodded. "Certainly," he agreed. "If you need me, you know where I'll be." He immediately headed out, understanding the gravity of their situation. As irritating as he could be, there was no doubt that he was an excellent guardian. They all were.

When Ivan and Alexander stepped closer to him, Ryker couldn't help but notice that they, too, scented him. And he didn't miss the small, puzzled look they exchanged. He didn't understand it, but he let it go. There would be plenty of time to ponder on it later.

The elevator dinged, signifying that someone from the lower level was about to make an appearance. The metal doors slid open, revealing Dr. Brown. Relief crossed his features when he saw Ryker. He stepped out, holding a folder in his hand.

"Ryker," he greeted him cordially. "I thought I might find you here. I've been trying to reach you at your home, but I haven't had any luck. I urgently need to talk to you, preferably alone."

"I've been in Alaska," Ryker replied, frowning. "Is there something wrong?"

Alexander cut them off. "Doctor Brown, we are actually in quite a bit of a hurry. We're leaving within the hour, and it's important that I brief Ryker. Is it critical? If it's anything less than life-threatening, I ask that you wait until we return before speaking with Ryker. Time really is of the essence, and we don't have much to play with."

"Certainly," Doctor Brown agreed, nodding his head. "Ryker, I'll speak with you when you return, but it is critical that I see you." The other man looked troubled, which made him uneasy.

"Very good," Alexander replied, clasping Ryker by the shoulder. He propelled him toward the hallway, leaving him no chance to question the doctor further. "In less than twenty-four hours we will be facing down some of the strongest werewolves in the world. If we expect to win, which I do, it's time to get down to business."

Chapter 14

Amanda woke up the following morning feeling terrible. She'd slept restlessly the night before, and it showed. Truth be told, she hadn't felt well since the day before, when they'd left the island. Then again, she hadn't had much rest. Between the amazing night she'd spent with Ryker, followed by the long flight and his departure, she was exhausted.

Forcing herself out of bed, she was surprised by how weak she felt. Come to think of it, she also felt ill and slightly feverish. The distance between the bed and bathroom seemed overwhelming, but nature was demanding that she make use of the facilities. Stumbling about, she went about her business. To her amazement, she succeeded.

Flopping back in bed, she rolled over to her side. She was scheduled to go into work that afternoon, and she really needed to be there. Considering the time she'd taken off, it was going to be a long day.

Her thoughts turned to Ryker, as they always did. The sex between them was outstanding. She was in love with him, of that she had no doubt. He made her feel things that she'd never experienced before. She could have easily spent a lifetime with him. It was too bad she wouldn't have the chance.

And he felt something for her, too. She was sure of it. Ryker cared enough about her to not want her to leave, and that was enough for her. Amanda knew her time left on Earth was limited, and she didn't want to waste her opportunity for love. Who knew how long she had left to enjoy it?

She said a quick prayer of thankfulness that the good Lord had blessed her by sending Ryker into her life. Her lifetime would be short, but she at least she could leave this world having experienced love. True love, not the sick, twisted relationship she'd experienced with Jimmy. Ryker actually cared about her, and it wasn't just sex. He'd provided a home and even a position for her, so she wouldn't feel as if she were taking without giving back. And by his actions, he'd relieved a lot of her fears and worries. Thanks to him and his consideration, she didn't have to die in fear, destitution, and worry over where she'd take her last breath. It was act of kindness so great she could never repay it – not even if she lived a thousand years.

For the first time in her adult life, Amanda actually knew what it felt like to be respected and cared for in a romantic relationship. The love she felt for Ryker really was awe-inspiring, the depth of her feelings knowing no boundaries. She couldn't say that he loved her, he'd made no mention of love, but the way he made her feel was considerable enough for her to be satisfied. At least for the limited time she had left. She wasn't going to walk away from him and lose him over three little words. Jimmy used to tell her he loved her, but had it been worth it? All he'd done was cheat, lie, and use her.

Ryker is worried I will leave. The thought left

her with a warm glow of pleasure. She was unused to anyone caring enough about her to worry over her actions. Knowing he did made her feel wanted. *Cherished.* She actually had a good man, but she was dying. She'd have to leave him behind, but at least she'd leave the world having experienced true passion and desire. The only thing sadder than dying at twenty-nine was dying without knowing what that felt like. *Thank you, Lord.*

Her thoughts were chaotic and all over the place, but so what? It wasn't everyday that a woman learned she was dying, especially at a point in her life where she should be living it to the fullest. On the crest of thirty, she should have been getting married or having babies, not making funeral plans. It would be easy to deny the truth, but denying or ignoring her impending demise would have served no helpful purpose. There were things she needed to do, and plans she needed to make. Starting with Jean.

She had no worldly possessions. The only thing she really owned was her beat up car. It was unlikely Jean would be able to sell it, but she could junk it and possibly get a few hundred bucks out of it. She wanted her to have it.

Amanda wanted to do something for Ryker, too, but what could you give the man that had it all? The paltry sum her car would bring wouldn't be worth it for him. With the economy, the bar was going through some tough times. Jean could use the money much more than Ryker could. No, for him she needed something different. Meaningful. She just didn't know what.

Ryker had assured her he'd be returning in the next few days. The thought left her with a pleasant glow, but she couldn't deny the twinge of worry she felt. Why, she didn't know. After all, hadn't he told her it was just a business trip? Still, something about it bothered her.

There was nothing she could do about it, though. He was gone, and she didn't know where. She just had to believe his promise to return and try to get through the next few days without him. She missed him more than she would have ever thought possible. Then again, she'd never loved anyone as much as she loved him. And when you loved someone you missed them when they were away. It was just the way it worked.

Her chest ached. She rubbed at it gently. It felt hard to breath, but Amanda dismissed it. The stress of the last two days was getting to her. Everything would be better when Ryker returned.

She dosed for a few hours before her alarm went off. Forcing herself to her feet, she dressed for work before heading to the bathroom. Amanda would have liked to showered, but it was too much effort. She felt too bad to even complete the simple task, so instead she washed her face and brushed her teeth. Even that exhausted her.

Her doctor's appointment was set for the following day. As bad as she felt, though, she wondered if she could even make it that long. He'd told her two months, though, and she was counting on surviving every one of those days. With that thought in mind, she left the house and drove to the bar.

Jean was smiling when she walked through the glass door, but her smile faded once she got a good look at her. "Amanda," she exclaimed, rushing around the end of the bar to assist her. "What in the hell has happened to you? You look like death. You shouldn't even be here today."

"I'm okay," Amanda replied, walking slowly. Now that she was a bookkeeper, she had her own special seat next to Jean. She'd been upgraded from the bar stool to a comfortable chair that actually swiveled. Jean had even cushioned it. She usually remained up front with the older woman while she did her work, using the surface of the bar as her desk. It suited them both.

"I haven't felt well all day," she admitted, once she slid into her seat. Jean watched her with a concerned expression on her face. "I'm going to see the doctor tomorrow, though. I should be okay to work on the books. I'd just as soon be here as I would at home. Ryker is away on a business trip."

"I wondered where he was at," Jean said, walking behind the bar to get her a glass of soda. She set it down in front of her with a straw. "The man usually follows you like a shadow. It's a nice feeling, huh? I remember the days. A man has to be really hooked to crave a woman's company like that."

Amanda smiled at her in appreciation, quickly sipping at the soda. Jean had put ice in it, and she quickly drank it down. She was thirstier than she had realized.

Jean watched her drink it, her hands spread on the bar as she frowned. "When's the last time you ate or drank anything?"

"Yesterday." It had been awhile. She should have got something from the house, but she just hadn't felt like it.

"That's not good, Amanda," Jean reprimanded her, in a stern voice. "You're going to have to take better care of yourself. In your condition it's easy to go down, and I mean quickly."

She turned to look over her shoulder at the clock before facing Amanda again. "I haven't had lunch yet. I'm going to call out for delivery. What do you want?"

They decided on pizza. After ordering, Jean went back to work while Amanda started on the books. The bar was quiet, with no customers in sight. It was an easy, familiar pattern.

The pizza delivery man came and went. The two women ate and talked about mundane things for awhile before Jean turned on the television. Pretty soon, the older woman got lost in her talk show.

By the time Amanda finished up her work, it was early evening. The nighttime bartender was there, well into her shift. Through the door, Amanda watched the setting sun. She dreaded the drive back to Ryker's house. She was dead tired, and she was still having a hard time breathing. Was she coming down with a cold? It was entirely possible.

Amanda slowly slid from the chair before leaning close to tell Jean goodbye. The bar was rapidly filling up, and the room was loud. She didn't have the energy to talk above the noise. "I'm going to head home now," she told the other woman, holding onto the edge of the chair while her legs adjusted to standing again.

Surprisingly, the older woman stood up, too. "I'm going to walk you out," Jean informed her, her voice leaving no room for argument. "And I want you to call me when you get home, just to let me know you made it. I don't feel right about you returning to an empty place."

"I'll be okay," Amanda replied automatically, stepping away from the bar. "I don't want you to worry about me."

"Someone needs to worry about you," Jean corrected her, holding the door open for her to pass through before following herself. Amanda shivered as she stepped out into the twilight. There was a definite chill in the air. Fall was definitely on its way.

Amanda turned back to face the older woman. Her side ached painfully. In the span of one day, she was literally falling apart. "Jean, I hate to ask you this," she told her humbly, embarrassed at the thought of imposing on the other woman. "I'm just not feeling that well. Do you think you could drive me to my doctor's appointment tomorrow?"

Nausea churned within her stomach. Her body flashed from cold to hot, as if it couldn't decide what temperature it wanted to be. She was going to have to leave, or she would embarrass herself.

"Of course," Jean replied, patting her on her arm. "It's no trouble at all."

Amanda nodded. "Thank you," she replied simply. "I'll call you in the morning with the appointment time."

"Don't forget to call me tonight, too," Jean called out as Amanda turned away. Amanda lifted her hand and waved in acknowledgment of Jean's words, but she didn't turn around. Instead she focused on placing one foot in the front of the other. If she could make it to the car, she could make it back to Ryker's house. Her sick, exhausted body needed to sit down.

But said body didn't cooperate with her plan of action. The pavement rushed up to meet her face as she fell, her head hitting the surface painfully. From somewhere far off Jean screamed her name, but Amanda was beyond responding. She coughed painfully, the unpleasant taste of blood lingering in her mouth. Had it come from her lungs or her face? She couldn't be sure.

Blackness hovered over her. Her chest felt like it was being crushed by a car. Every breath was a struggle. She was too weak to even roll over, so she remained where she was, face down on the ground. She was in trouble, and she realized it.

"Amanda," Jean screamed again, her voice hoarse. It barely penetrated the fog that surrounded her. "She's unresponsive," Jean yelled to someone behind them, squatting down to shake her shoulder. "Tell the dispatcher to get an ambulance out here fast, or there will be hell to pay."

"Help me roll her over." Fingers dug into Amanda's body, tugging insistently. The pain was horrendous. A choked sob escaped her lips, but it wasn't loud. She felt weak, as if every bit of strength had been leeched from her body. She also felt panic, it was impossible not to.

Several faces stared down at her. "Oh, my God," Jean wailed, her wrinkled hands gently touching her face. "We're getting you help, Amanda," she said, a sheen of tears in her eyes. "The ambulance is on the way."

Someone lowered her down to the ground, flat on her back. The pressure on her chest increased, her eyes widening from fear. The air left her weakened lungs, her body too ravaged to draw in her next breath. She was suffocating in front of their very eyes, and nobody even realized it.

In her mind she yelled and thrashed, but in actuality her body barely twitched. Her scream was little more than a strangled rush of air, but it was enough. "Get her up," Jean yelled, quickly grabbing her hands as she pulled. "Something is wrong with her lungs. She's not breathing."

Amanda's eyes closed in relief when she felt

hands lifting her into a seated position. The pain was horrible, but at least she could breath. Blood dripped from her nose and mouth, running down her face and clothing. *I was choking to death on my own secretions*, she realized in horror. *What is happening to me?*

She continued to hover at the edge of consciousness, easily hearing everything that was said around her but not strong enough to speak. And in the parking lot of a bar, surrounded by intoxicated strangers, she fought for her every breath as they unselfishly did everything they could to keep her alive.

"Go get my purse and phone," Jean ordered her newest bartender, still holding Amanda's hands. Someone sat behind her, using their body to hold hers upright. "And close the bar up. I'm going with her in the ambulance. I won't have her going through this alone."

In the distance, Amanda heard the sirens. *Just a little bit longer.* She didn't know what was wrong with her, but she was scared of dying before she had the chance to tell Ryker goodbye. In their capable hands, though, surely they could keep her alive long enough for him to return. *They have to.*

The ambulance pulled into the parking lot. The next several minutes passed by in a flurry of painful activity as the paramedics loaded her in.

And throughout it all, nobody noticed the man dressed in black as he stood next to the trees.

* * * * *

The sheik stepped back into the woods as the

ambulance pulled out, frowning heavily as he pondered on his discovery... and what he should do about it.

The human female was Ryker's mate, of that he had no doubt. She fairly reeked of him, even from across the parking lot. What he couldn't understand, though, was why his fellow comrade had not claimed her. Obviously she was ill. Was her illness enough to prevent the mating, or had it been something else?

Before arriving at the bar, he hadn't known that Ryker had mated. But the wolf that lived within him did, and he had called him to this time and place, just like he always did. After all, as sheik it was his job to monitor the newly mated females. The man he was might not know when he was needed, but the wolf always did. It was his position within the pack.

Was it possible that Ryker was unaware that the female was his mate? The sheik didn't see how, but stranger things had happened. If that were the case, he had a responsibility to watch over and protect her until the other man could.

What he needed was information, and there was only one way to get it. Moving swiftly through the trees, he followed the ambulance. Once he knew what was wrong, he'd be in a better position to deliver the solution. He just hoped the female lived long enough for Ryker to get back to her for he'd scented the acrid smell of death... and it had fully surrounded her.

Chapter 15

Their jeeps ground to a halt, their headlights turning off. It left the desert in complete darkness, but that mattered little to the guardians. They could see their rugged surroundings perfectly.

The area around the crater was packed full of vehicles, and werewolves were everywhere. The challenge had drawn people from every pack around the world. All of them would be affected by the outcome of the match, and they knew it. The entire future of the werewolves would be decided within the next hour. The very air was thrumming with tension.

Ryker knew most of them hoped that Alexander would win, but some of the packs were foolish enough to hope that Balor had victory. They were idiots. Under Alexander's rule, they'd known peace and safety. Balor was rash and outspoken and too prone to impulsive decisions. Under his rule, the werewolves faced discovery and eventual extinction.

Several wolves from the Australian pack walked up to them, their expressions smug and cocky. They escorted them through the darkness without speaking to them, which suited Ryker just fine. He was royally pissed. Because of them, he'd been forced to leave Amanda behind. He couldn't wait to bust some heads.

The ground surrounding the crater was extremely rocky, but the terrain was flat. They followed the wolves up the incline and to the rim, all of them stopping to stare down. Spread out across the crater was one of the largest cages Ryker had ever seen. Not only were the walls caged off, but so was the top. The Australian pack was out for blood, but they were going to regret being caged in once Alexander and Ryker stepped inside.

Connor cleared his throat, rubbing his hands together in anticipation. "How nice of you boys," he drawled out to the werewolf closest to him. "By setting up the cage like this, our contenders won't have to worry about one of you babies running off. I might as well break out the beers now. This match is all but over with. Only a moron would lock himself into a wire cage with Alexander or Ryker."

The Australian werewolf snarled at him silently, but he didn't engage Connor. It was a smart move. Connor was mouthy, but he was an excellent fighter. The other wolf wouldn't have stood a chance.

As they stood at the rim, the area came alive with floodlights. The crowd immediately quieted. Ryker muscles thickened in anticipation. Things were about to get dangerous. He couldn't wait.

A fellow werewolf stepped out into the spotlights, a microphone in his hand. Tall and thickly-built, he looked calm and confident as he held it to his mouth. "Brothers and sisters, my name is Lucas. By now, most of you know the reason for this match, so I'm not going to delay it with needless explanations. Instead, I'm going to explain the rules, and then our competitors will fight."

The crowd went wild. Lucas held up a hand to stop them. "In the challenges of old, there was only one fighter on each side, unless the seconds were called in. That's too tame for us, so we're going to change it up a bit. In this match, all four men will be in the ring. The winning pack will have to defeat both the first and the second in order to succeed as king. And when I say defeat, I mean kill. Only one side will be walking back out of that cage, or none at all. There is no middle ground."

He continued to talk, but it wasn't anything important. Alexander looked at Ryker, his expression grim. "I'm sorry you have to be pulled into this," he told him, his expression angry. "I didn't think you'd actually have to fight. I should have known they'd have some type of trick up their sleeve."

Ryker just shrugged. "No worries," he muttered, rolling his shoulders back in a circle. "Let's just kick some ass and get back home."

Marrok was standing on Alexander's other side, his expression solemn. Alexander paused for a moment, staring down at the cage as if he were considering his next words. "Marrok, I want you to keep Ivan on speakerphone, so he's aware of everything that's happening. Should I fail, he will know what to do."

"He's already on the line," Marrok replied, gesturing toward his hip. His cell phone was clipped at his lean waist.

"Good, I should have known you'd be on top of

things. You always are." Alexander clapped him on the back, his expression resigned.

Ryker turned toward the men, his own thoughts heavy. "I'd like to make a request of you, too, Marrok, if I may," he said to the other man, much to everyone's surprise. Ryker ignored them. "If something should happen to me, I want you to tell Amanda that I love her." It was brief and to the point.

The other guardians gaped at him, but none of them cracked a joke. Instead they watched him with grave expressions on their faces as if they understood. "She might not be my mate, but I love her as if she were. Given a bit more time, I would have made our relationship official. I can't imagine caring about any female more than I do her. She means everything to me, but if I can't be there to care for her I want the pack to treat her as if she were mine. Protect her and watch over her, please."

"Of course we would," Connor told him. "I know we've had our disagreements in the past, but I hope you haven't taken them personally. I give everyone a hard time. It's just my nature."

Ryker nodded, turning to watch the activity in the crater. "It's time for our contestants to enter the cage," Lucas said, his voice booming over the speakers. "Up first, we have Balor and Oliver... from the Australian pack."

The two men entered the ring, both of them tall and massive. They were even taller than Ryker, which meant they'd all but dwarf Alexander. None of the men were short, but the other two males were well over seven feet tall.

"That's our cue," Alexander said wryly, quickly undressing. Ryker followed suit, leaving his clothing in a pile. As werewolves, they were expected to fight nude. It was likely that they'd change into their wolf forms at some point, clothing would only hamper them.

They walked down the incline and into the crater, both of them silent. At the gate they waited as they perused the competition. In order to win, they would have to take both men down. "I'm going after Balor," Ryker whispered, speaking carefully so he wouldn't be overheard. "Between the both of us, I'm the tallest. Oliver isn't quite as tall as Balor, which will make you more evenly matched."

Alexander nodded, his eyes scanning the cage. "Remember, our only goal is to take them down. They will want to show off a little bit, but we're going straight for the kill. Stay alert for any tricks; I don't trust the Australian pack. They might try to surprise us with something extra, especially if they think the fight is going in our favor."

Ryker didn't have a chance to respond. "And now we have Alexander and Ryker, from the Missouri pack," Lucas announced grandly as the cage opened again.

The roar from the crowd was deafening. A small smile played about Alexander's lips as he entered. He was pleased to have the support, but why wouldn't he? Alexander had always done right by the werewolves, they couldn't have asked for a better king.

After both men were in, the gate closed behind them. Ryker perused the crowd, immediately spotting several guardians scattered within their depths. They were surrounded by members of their own pack, which reassured him. Alert and cautious, the guardians were on guard. They wouldn't allow any interference from outside of the cage. Ryker and Alexander just had to watch out for anything within it.

"Competitors, you know what to do," Lucas yelled, finishing up. "At the horn, you may begin."

Ryker and Alexander remained on one end of the cage, while Balor and Oliver remained on the other. They sized each other up, each team looking for weaknesses in their opponents. All of them remained in human form, but that could and would change at a second's notice.

The Australians hadn't bothered covering the ground when they'd set up the cage, but it had probably been done intentionally. It was sandy and rocky, which would make the fight more difficult. The rocks were different sizes and many of them had jagged edges. It wouldn't bother them in wolf form, but it certainly could as humans.

The horn blew, its sound loud in the suddenly quiet night. Thousands of eyes were trained on them, some of them in support while others were anticipating their defeat. Balor and Oliver approached them at a dead run, but Alexander and Ryker remained completely still.

Three. Two. One! When Balor was only steps away Ryker jumped, grabbing the top of the cage and holding on. At the same time, his foot connected with the other man's face, knocking him clear off his feet. He slid across the uneven surface of the crater's floor before coming to a stop. He leaped back to his feet as Ryker dropped down to the ground.

"Damn, that really had to hurt," Ryker taunted him, enjoying Balor's expression. "You're going to be digging rocks out of your ass for a long time, huh?"

A scream broke through the silence of the night. Alexander clearly had Oliver in hand. While Ryker went high, Alexander had gone low. Oliver was attempting to fight the king with one hand shielded protectively over his crotch area. In other words, he was getting his ass whipped.

Ryker danced away from the other two men, leading Balor away from Alexander. He didn't want him that close to Alexander's unsuspecting back. A lot could happen pretty quickly, when it was two against one.

Balor smiled at him, his face more animal than human. Everything was big about the other man, well, almost everything. Ryker's eyes widened when he happened to get a glimpse at the area between his legs. "Holy shit," he told Balor, eying him with disgust. "Damn, what the fuck happened to you? Was the doctor drunk when he circumcised you or something? You must be a hit with the virgins. A woman could bed you and still be untouched, even after you've given it your best shot."

His words enraged the other man. He launched his body at him with the speed of a train, immediately going for Ryker's neck. But Ryker had anticipated it. He kneed him hard in the stomach, and when Balor bent over he grabbed him by the throat and hair, preparing to rip his head off.

His move left Balor's hands free. A large, meaty fist slammed into Ryker's side, breaking his ribs instantly. The blow stunned Ryker enough for Balor to break free. He skirted around him before charging again.

The fight continued, with neither side making any real progress. All four men were bruised and bloodied. They needed to end the match and quickly. It was too dangerous to continue, there was always the possibility that one of the Australians would gain the upper hand.

Alexander was on the opposite side of the cage, fully engaged with Oliver. Ryker jabbed Balor in the stomach before catching him underneath the chin with an uppercut. The other man remained standing.

"Where's a two by four when you need one?" Ryker muttered, kicking out at the other man. His foot connected with Balor's knee, and this time he did go down. He landed next to a log. When he came back up, he held something in his hand.

"I'm getting real sick of you, pretty boy," Balor sneered at him, his weapon held out in a menacing manner. "Why don't you just admit defeat? You're going to die anyhow."

Ryker glared at him as he said coldly, "Hiding behind weapons now? Why don't you be a real man and fight me with your hands instead of cheating? Using that will only get you disqualified."

Balor laughed, revealing fangs. "Disqualified? I think not. Did you hear Lucas say that weapons weren't allowed?" He advanced toward Ryker, his face filled with glee. "I think not," he continued, answering his own question. "Besides, what do you think everyone else sees? I'll tell you what. They see me holding a rock, nothing more. None of them would ever think this weapon had been specially created for this event, and they'd certainly never guess that it was lined with silver."

Ryker eyed him with disgust. The knife was made out of a reddish-orange material, just like the rocks around them. Alexander's suspicions had been correct. The Australian wolves had set them up. And they'd done it rather cleverly, making sure that their weapons would look like something natural, when in truth they were anything but.

Up close, he could see the handle. Balor was careful to avoid any contact with the blade. Silver was extremely painful to a werewolf, which was why the other wolf was using it. He knew it would render Ryker incapable, at least long enough for Balor to finish him off.

He needed to warn Alexander before Oliver

retrieved one of his own. It was likely they had them stowed all over the crater, within easy access when they needed them. "Well, I guess you're only half a man inside and out," Ryker said, crouching in preparation of Balor's attack. "And I don't think there's enough man inside of you to take me down. So bring your little weapon and your little dick and do your best. Your bitchy attitude is seriously starting to bore me."

Balor came at him with a roar, slashing out with everything he had in him. Ryker danced around him, careful to keep away from the blade. He punched him every chance he got, but he needed more than that. A punch wasn't enough to bring him down.

Gasps of horror and outrage filled the air. Ryker looked past Balor to Alexander, horrified to see the blade embedded in his stomach. Using the handle, Oliver wrenched it up as hard as he could, in an effort to inflict the most damage.

Balor quickly glanced behind him. Realizing that his pack mate had brought the king down, he began to laugh. "Well, looks like you're a dead man now," he informed Ryker, advancing on him step by step. "Not that I ever doubted it."

Ryker roared loudly, the veins on his neck protruding in rage. This time, he didn't wait for Balor to attack first. Instead he slammed into him, taking him down to the ground with his body.

His fists pummeled into the other man's face, his knees holding Balor's hands down to his sides with the weight of his body. Balor bucked hard, freeing one hand. He used it to knock Ryker to the side before quickly coming to his feet.

Ryker followed suit, but he was an instant too late. Balor slammed him in the head with a large rock, knocking him back down to the ground. He quickly grabbed him by the hair, pulling him to his feet with the knife held at his throat. "Say hello to your king," he spat out at him. "I hope you both rot in hell."

With only one option left, Ryker shifted. As soon as his back legs hit the ground, he rotated and leaped at the same time, catching Balor in the throat with his wide jaws. He didn't hesitate. In one satisfying crunch, he ripped out half his throat. With the next bite Balor's spinal cord broke, his head separating from his body. He died immediately.

Ryker spat as he shifted, disgusted by the taste of the other male in his mouth. He set off at a dead run toward the other end of the cage, relieved to see Alexander standing. Despite the gaping wound in his abdomen, the other man was still fighting. He was weakening, though, it was there in his delayed hits and abnormally pale skin. He needed care from a doctor and fast, or there was no chance in hell he'd survive.

A few feet away from the other men Ryker jumped, clearing the distance easily. He slammed into Oliver's back, taking him down to the ground. In Oliver's hand was the knife he'd used on Alexander. Ryker slammed a fist into the back of his arm, smiling at the satisfying crunch as the other man released the knife.

"You bastard," Ryker yelled, watching as Alexander weakly tried to stay on his feet. "You brought your own death upon yourself, remember that. You chose this the instant you forced us into this challenge, and my king will be vindicated." And with that he grabbed Oliver's hair and brought the long blade down, separating his head from his body in one swoop.

Ryker came to his feet, moving to stand next to Alexander, but he didn't try to support him. Assisting him in front of the others would have only been a sign of weakness. Alexander wouldn't have appreciated the gesture. So instead he muttered, "Just hang on. We'll be out of here in moments."

At first, the rim remained quiet, as if the spectators couldn't really believe it was over. But then it erupted in cheers, the crowd chanting their names. The challenge was over, but would Alexander survive it? He needed help not cheers. But it was unlikely that anyone outside of the Australian pack realized that silver had been used on their king.

Connor and Marrok moved to stand at the fence, their expressions concerned. "Why isn't Alexander healing?" Connor hissed, keeping his voice low.

"He was stabbed with a silver blade," Ryker replied, out of the corner of his mouth. "Apparently, the Australians have plenty of them hidden out here. They designed them to look like shards of rock so the other packs wouldn't find out. We need to get out of here. Find Doctor Sanders and let him know what's happened."

Connor nodded before slipping away, leaving Marrok behind. The other man turned his back to them, his watchful eyes scanning the crowd.

"There you have it," Lucas announced on the microphone. "Alexander and Ryker have won the challenge, and Alexander will retain his role as King of Wolves." With a renewed burst of energy, the crowd cheered even louder.

The gate was unlocked. Ryker and Alexander turned to walk out, both men taking their time. Alexander held his head high as he left the cage, his pride evident to all. The man was not only born to lead, he'd proven it with the challenge. Ryker doubted anyone would be foolish enough to challenge him again.

The doctor was waiting outside the gate, his expression concerned. Once outside the cage, Alexander stumbled. He would have fallen had Ryker and Connor not grabbed him. Maintaining his pride had come at a price, but the king had made the right choice. It would have been a mistake to show weakness while still in the cage. He was out now, though. They just needed to get him away from the crater before the well-wishers descended on him to offer their congratulations.

The two men held him up while Doctor Sanders quickly inspected his wound. "We need to get him out of here and back to the plane as soon as possible," he informed them, staring at them with an uneasy expression on his face. "I need to clean his wound out, but I don't want to do it here. I don't trust this pack, not after what they did."

Ryker nodded in agreement. "What's the best way to get him out?"

"One of our guardians is bringing a jeep to the base of the rim in front of us," Marrok informed them. "Orlando and I will go in front of you, and the other guardians are moving into position now. They'll hold off the crowd while you two get him to the jeep. After that, I've ordered them to evacuate the crater as soon as possible." He stared at the cage with a look of disgust. "I don't see any need for us to delay, do you?"

"Hell, no," Ryker responded, shaking his head. "The sooner we get out of here the better. It's a pity. Up until this shit, I'd always liked Australia. I doubt I'll be back anytime soon, though."

"If I survive this, I'm going to take action against this pack," Alexander said, through clenched teeth. He had a sheen of sweat on his forehead, and his coloring was off. "What they did was dirty and underhanded. They will be reprimanded."

The men assisted Alexander outside of the crater and into the jeep. Doctor Sanders and Marrok climbed into the back. "I'm going to hitch a ride to the plane with Orlando," Ryker informed them, taking his clothing out of the younger guardian's arms with a smile of gratitude. "It was a good fight, my liege," he told Alexander directly. "Thank you for the honor of being your second."

"No, thank you," Alexander replied from the front seat, his face wan. "You saved my life. I won't forget that."

"There will be time to talk later," Doctor Sanders informed them sternly. "If we get a move on."

Ryker nodded, stepping back from the jeep to watch it pull away. Now that the challenge was over, it would appear that everyone was ready to depart. He hoped that they made it back to the plane quickly. The sheer amount of vehicles driving away was staggering.

He quickly dressed, his thoughts on Amanda. He was eager to get back to Missouri and eager to start his life with her. He was going to reveal everything to her, including the fact that he was a werewolf. Ryker felt confident that she wouldn't resist the change. Why would she? Turning into a werewolf would resolve all of their problems, including her cancer. He'd never have to worry about losing her to another human ailment again.

"I'm going to round up one of the other jeeps so we can get out of here," Orlando told him, looking back and forth for someone he knew. "This place blows."

The phone rang in his pocket, signaling an incoming call. "I'll be waiting," he told Orlando, pulling the phone out of his pocket. "I've got a call. Just let me know when it's time to head out." Orlando nodded, disappearing in the crowd.

Ryker looked down at the caller id, frowning when he saw the number was blocked. A sense of foreboding washed over him. The guardians never blocked their numbers when they called each other. Only someone that wanted to remain unidentified would do so, and that didn't bode well for his upcoming call.

"Ryker Connell," he stated briskly into the phone. "Who are you, and why is your number blocked?"

"My reasons for blocking my number aren't important," a low male voice told him. "But my reason for calling is."

As hard as he tried Ryker couldn't place the voice, but he knew he'd heard it before. "And what is the reason you're calling?" he asked him, willing to play his game, at least for the moment.

"The human female that resides with you is in trouble," the man continued, in a flat voice. Ryker wondered if he spoke that way naturally, or if it was an attempt to disguise his voice. Either way, it was pretty effective. "I know that the challenge ended, and it was won in your favor. The female's time is drawing near, though, and she won't last here on this mortal plane for long."

"What are you talking about?" Ryker hissed into the phone, his very blood freezing in his veins. "Who the hell are you, and what do you know about Amanda? So help me if you've harmed her, I will kill you myself."

"I haven't touched her," the voice replied coolly. "But something within her has. Death is hovering all around her, just waiting to catch her up in its unrelenting clutch. She's in a coma at Nashoba Memorial, and now you know. What you choose to do with that knowledge is up to you."

"Wait," Ryker yelled into the phone, but it was too late. The caller had hung up. He spun around in a panic, looking for Orlando. In the distance, he spotted the other man. He was talking to a guardian, right next to an empty jeep.

Ryker slid the phone into his pocket and took off at a dead run, his long legs quickly eating up the distance. Orlando stared at him in shock as he jumped into the driver's seat, climbing in himself as Ryker started it up. "Dude, what the hell?" Orlando asked, quickly strapping in as Ryker threw it into reverse. "Where are you going?"

Ryker shifted into drive as he floored the accelerator, rocks and dirt flying everywhere. He dodged around the parked vehicles as he headed down the bumpy road, determined to leave Australia as quickly as possible. "Amanda is in a coma," he explained, dodging a pothole. "I need you to call Marrok or Connor and tell them we have to leave immediately."

"Oh, shit!" Orlando screamed, his eyes widening in panic. The other guardian had missed his calling, he could have easily starred in an opera. A car swerved around them as they blew their horn. Ryker ignored the finger that was extended in his direction. "Dude, you're driving on the wrong side of the road," Orlando informed him, gripping the dashboard. "We're in Australia. You're supposed to be on the left side, not the right."

"Whatever," Ryker grumbled, but he did switch sides. "Now make that call." If what his caller said was true, there was every possibility that he wouldn't make it back in time, even if he left right away. He roared in frustration.

Orlando was on the phone with one of the guardians. "Yeah, that was Ryker," he said into the phone, shooting Ryker an uncomfortable glance. "The dude is seriously fucked up. He stole a jeep, nearly ran over Kyle, and he almost killed us in a head-on collision. I don't know what the hell has happened, but he says that Amanda is in a coma." Orlando conveniently ignored the glare that Ryker sent him, falling silent as he listened to the voice on the other end of the line.

"I'll tell him," Orlando finally said. "Maybe that will calm him down enough to get us back there safely. If I don't make it, though, please don't tell my mother I died from Ryker's bad driving. Make it sound good and tell her I died in the line of duty. At least that way she'll be proud."

Ryker snarled at Orlando, but he didn't notice. He hung up the phone before turning to look at Ryker. "A plane will be ready to leave as soon as we arrive. Alexander will be with us. From what Connor just said, he's not doing very well."

Chapter 16

Ryker stalked down the hallway of Nashoba Memorial, oblivious to the stares from those around him. He knew what they saw as they watched him. With his build, beard shadow, and wrinkled clothing he looked every bit of the dangerous werewolf he was. But at least he wasn't feral. Not yet.

The flight had seemed to take forever. Between the stops to refuel and delays due to the weather, it had taken them twenty hours to make it back to Missouri. Ryker had been the first one off the plane, leaping off before the stairs had even been pushed to the door. He'd landed in a crouch before taking off in the direction of the hospital at a dead run, ignoring the shouts from behind him as the guardians offered to drive him.

Jean sat in a line of chairs against the wall. She raised her head as Ryker walked up to her, her eyes teary. The woman looked ten years older than she had the last time he'd seen her. "Which room?" he asked, wasting no time on greetings.

"In there," she said, pointing at the closed door just a few feet away from her. "She's not alone, though. Her sister is in there, with the doctor."

Her mouth ground together in one flat line as she stopped to swallow hard. "She's not doing very well, Ryker," she finally told him, her voice trembling in pain. "Amanda is in a coma. She's been unresponsive since a little bit after the ambulance brought her in, and the doctors say that the cancer has spread to her lungs, liver, and brain. She's already flat lined once, so they put her on a ventilator. She can't breathe on her own."

Ryker's hands clenched into his fists, he had to fight to hold in the pain instead of roaring out his grief. He wasn't sure if he wanted to fall to his knees or bust out a wall. A thousand emotions slammed into his body like a punch in the gut. He couldn't handle it, but he had to. He had to fix it, he had to fix her. "I'm going in."

Pushing the metal lever to open the wooden door, he shoved it open wide as he stepped in. Her scent rushed over him, everything sweet, good, and pure, and in that moment his entire world was rocked over on its side as he made a startling discovery. Amanda *was* his mate, and she had been all along. The chemotherapy had masked her scent, but it hadn't wholly eradicated it. She was his, not only by his own declaration, but by fate itself. And there was no force on Earth powerful enough to separate him from her. Ever.

"Excuse me," the doctor said irritably, his lip curled up as gave Ryker the once over. "Who are you, and why are you in here?"

A woman stood next to him, staring at Ryker with interest. Although she didn't resemble Amanda, Ryker could scent the familial bond between them. Something about her put him off immediately. He couldn't be sure if it was the teased hair or the indifference in her eyes when she stared at her sister, but he didn't like her. She was nothing like Amanda. No wonder they weren't close.

"I'm her fiance," he shot back in a hard voice, sending the doctor a look that dared him to try and put him out. "And I want to know what the hell has happened, and how you're going to fix it." It was an order not a question, and all three of them knew it.

"Fiance, hmm?" Amanda's sister drawled, staring between him and the women in the bed. "Wow, how the hell was she ever lucky enough to land something that looks like you?"

Ryker sent her a dismissive glance before walking over to stand next to the hospital bed. He wanted to cry out in anguish at his first sight of Amanda. Her face was bruised and swollen on one side, and she had residual dried spots of blood on her on her neck and head. Her mouth was open due to the ventilator, her beautiful blue eyes closed. Someone had removed her wig, revealing the soft regrowth of hair that surrounded her head. "What happened to her face?" he asked, in a voice that was more animal than human. He turned his head to look at the doctor.

The doctor stared back at him, his own eyes widening at the expression on Ryker's face. "She collapsed in a parking lot," the doctor answered him, in a nervous squeak. "From my understanding, it happened where she works."

Ryker turned back to Amanda, continuing his tally of her injuries. With trembling hands he reached out to touch her, his fingers lightly resting on her face. She'd lost so much weight that his hands seemed to engulf her head. Her skin was cold to the touch, but what worried him the most was that she felt stiff. *Like her body is already caught in the throes of death.*

Her chest jerked unnaturally, keeping in time with the machine that was sustaining her fragile life. Underneath the neckline of the hospital gown, she had a rash across her chest, the red bumps at odds with her porcelain pale skin. Running his palm down her arm, he stopped when he felt wetness. Glancing down, he growled at the sight of her swollen arms and hands. With his supernatural vision, he could see the numerous microscopic holes in her arms. She'd been poked with a needle, too many times to count.

Ryker spun around, glaring at the doctor. "You call this care?" he asked in disbelief, gesturing back to Amanda. "Her arms are swollen to twice their regular size, and they are leaking." He made a rude sound of disgust in the back of his throat, angered that she'd been treated so carelessly. "No wonder she's in a coma, if this is what you call medical treatment."

"Amanda has a severe case of sepsis," the doctor informed him. He walked up to the hospital bed in a brave show of professionalism, stopping to stare down at his patient. "It's a severe infection that attacks the kidneys, lungs, and skin, and it's not uncommon in those with weakened immune systems, such as people undergoing chemotherapy."

The doctor lifted Amanda's arm, gently

inspecting it before placing it back down on the sheet. "It's also one of the most deadly infections," he admitted, meeting Ryker's eyes. "Despite our best efforts, she's moved into septic shock, and we are having problems keeping an IV line in her veins. Her arms are swollen due to the fluids we've been treating her with, and we are running out of veins to try."

"How the hell is any of this helping, then?" Ryker demanded. "If the IV line isn't staying in the vein, clearly the antibiotics aren't hitting it either." Instead they were leaking out onto the sheets, from the numerous holes in her arms.

"You're right," the doctor admitted, sighing heavily. "And there's nothing else that we can do for her except pray. She's awfully young, but I've learned in my years of practice that age doesn't necessarily matter. Over the years I've watched the young die just as easily as the elderly, and I've seen the elderly experience medical miracles just as much as the young. Cases like these are always the hardest, and as a doctor I've never grown immune to it. Dying from sepsis isn't an easy death. If we could have got to it sooner, it might have made a difference. It's a very hard illness for the average person to recognize, though. It's often misdiagnosed as a bladder infection or bronchitis, at least until it has reached a severe level.

Ryker nodded bleakly, taking it all in. As sick as she was, he wasn't even sure he'd be able to change her. He had to talk to a pack doctor, the sooner the better.

"In addition to the coma, Amanda also has pneumonia, kidney failure, and we're fighting to keep her blood pressure up," the doctor continued, putting it all out on the table for Ryker. "She's flat lined once, and we resuscitated her. It's likely to happen again, and I need to know how you'd like to proceed, if it does."

"What do you mean?" Ryker asked, staring down at the doctor with a disgusted expression on his face. "Are you asking if I would allow you to pull the plug on Amanda? Hell, no," he spat out, moving away from the doctor before he decked him. "I expect you to do everything within your power to bring her back."

"Actually, I wasn't asking you," the doctor replied, turning his head to face Amanda's sister. "I understand your position as her fiance, but you aren't married. That means her sister is her next of kin, and she's the one responsible for making her medical decisions. If the two of you need time to talk about this, I can leave. You can always inform the nurse of your decision."

"I don't give a shit if you're talking to me or not. I'm talking to you, and in my book that's all that matters." It took everything he had to control himself. "Are you saying there's no possibility that she'll wake up again?"

The doctor looked exasperated. "It's highly unlikely that she will. Even if she did, though, it would only be temporary. We are treating the infection, but we can't treat the cancer. She's terminal."

"And you don't think that brief amount of time might actually mean something to her?" Ryker asked incredulously. "You'd begrudge her the right to be alive for as long as possible? I don't see where either one of you gets off on making that type of decision for her. She has cancer, but so what? Deciding to end her life without her approval is wrong. If she would have wanted this, she would have left it in writing. God knows she had plenty of opportunity to."

"All of this bickering isn't necessary," Amanda's sister replied, waving her arm dismissively. She wore a ton of golden hued bracelets. They jingled together in an irritating symphony of noise. "From my understanding, there is no reasonable expectation of her recovery. Even if somehow the infection is cured, she still has cancer. There really is no choice to make. I want her removed from the ventilator and all life support stopped. Tonight."

"You selfish bitch," Ryker yelled, swinging his arm toward the door. "It'll be a cold day in hell before I let you get away with that. What a pity that Amanda had to be stuck with you as a sister. And you," he told the doctor as he saw him backing away. "Don't even think about taking her off this machine. I'm calling my attorneys tonight. By the time they're done with you and this hospital, there won't be anything left to run this place with. Now, get the hell out here before I really get pissed off."

Both of them rushed the door, desperate to get away from him. In seconds they were gone, leaving the room in blessed silence. He was completely furious over their attempts to end her life. He had to get her out of the hospital and quickly.

Had she been able to breathe without the machine, he would have taken her out the window. She couldn't, though. It was a problem too big for him to handle on his own. Grabbing his cell phone, he dialed headquarters.

"Doctor Brown," he said gravely, when the other man came on the line. "It's Ryker. Amanda is in Nashoba Memorial... and I need your help."

*****

Ryker rubbed a weary hand over his face before leaning forward to rest his arms on his knees. He was two levels down at headquarters, sitting in the small waiting area outside of the patient's rooms. He wasn't alone. Headquarters had been packed the entire night. Between Alexander and Amanda, Wolf Town's doctors were very busy.

He hadn't been there long. After his previous call with Doctor Brown, the other man had shown up at Nashoba Memorial with an ambulance. He'd pulled some strings and arranged Amanda's release. Her sister was nowhere to be found.

Doctor Brown had discovered that she'd already signed the paperwork that was needed to end Amanda's life. She'd also given explicit instructions for Amanda to be cremated, without even the courtesy of a visitation or funeral. Believing that she'd effectively tied up her loose ends, she was already on her way out of town. *What a bitch.*

Jean was another story, though. The older woman had been waiting when he'd stepped outside of Amanda's room. And she'd remained until they left. Ryker hadn't been able to tell her the full truth, but he'd told her enough to reassure her. When the ambulance pulled out of the parking lot, Ryker hadn't missed the gratitude and relief within her pain-filled eyes. Jean wasn't related to Amanda, but she loved her like a grandmother loved her grandchild.

Doctor Brown and Doctor Sanders were the two lead doctors at Wolf Town. Both men were currently examining Amanda and talking amongst themselves as they came to an agreement on the best way to proceed. They knew Ryker was more than willing to change her, but it would have to be handled carefully. She was in a very delicate position, her weakened body barely holding on. The seconds passed like hours as he waited impatiently for them to deliver their verdict.

"The sun is coming up," Ivan told him, from the chair next to him. "Of course I can't see it from down here, but I can feel it. Isn't it weird how in-tune with nature our bodies are? But I have to admit there isn't a day that goes by that I'm not grateful to be a werewolf."

Ryker gave him a sideways glance out of the corner of his eyes, bemused by the other man's chatter. Was he just making small talk or babbling from exhaustion? God, who knew. Everyone was worried and exhausted.

The older werewolf didn't seem to expect a response, so Ryker remained silent.

Ivan shifted in his seat before rubbing the back of his neck with his hand. "And take my grandson, Alexander. He wasn't only stabbed in the stomach, he was gutted. It was a wound that would have killed your average human, regardless of whatever type of medical treatment they received. But not him, and it wasn't just because he's a werewolf. He not only survived a fatal wound, but he survived a twenty-hour flight back to his family and wife. Alexander is a survivor and so is your mate. She's hung on long enough for you to get back to her, and now she's in good hands."

The door opened. Both doctors stepped out quietly, moving to stand in front of Ivan and Ryker. "Your mate is settled and stable for now," Doctor Sanders informed Ryker, his eyebrows pulled together. "You'll be able to join her once we're done talking."

"Nashoba Memorial gave us a copy of her medical records on a disc," Doctor Brown added. "We've reviewed them to make sure they didn't miss any additional conditions. They didn't. Surprisingly, they were very thorough in their tests and procedures. We did some blood work on Amanda, but unfortunately her white blood cell count has only increased, which means the infection is getting worse."

"I need to change her, then," Ryker interrupted, coming to his feet. "I should do it now."

"We think it's not too late to do so," Doctor Brown said, holding up a hand to stop him. "*We think.* In all my years, I don't believe I've seen someone changed so close to death, though. Even worse, she's weak. A long-term illness like cancer destroys a person's organs. Once she's changed, the wolf will try to repair all that, but will Amanda have enough resources within her to sustain her wolf while it does so? None of can say, but the answer to that will determine whether or not she survives the conversion."

"But that's not all." Doctor Sanders looked concerned, as if he feared the other doctor would leave out something vital. "Amanda is too far gone to agree to the change. We all know what that means."

Oh, shit. With everything that had happened, Ryker had never considered that. Nature almost always required a person's willingness in order to convert them into a werewolf. Without Amanda's consent, there was a very good chance that her body wouldn't accept the change. It was nature's way of protecting the weaker species, and overall, it was pretty damned effective. Most werewolves would never consider changing anyone without their approval. It would have been pointless, if the other person didn't survive it.

Defeat and helplessness washed over Ryker in waves. He hung his head, completely grieved over the very real possibility of losing Amanda. "If I don't change her, she will die," he said out loud. "Yet if I do change her, she could still die. How the hell is any mate supposed to go up against odds like that?"

The room was silent as Ivan and the two doctors awaited his decision. It was the hardest one he'd ever had to make, but he couldn't let her go without a fight. He raised his head, meeting their eyes. "If she has to die, she won't do it without at least having a chance. We're going to change her, but know this. If Amanda dies, I do, too. I have no desire to live in a world without her. I won't do it."

"All right, then," Doctor Brown said, clapping his hands together. There was no censure in his eyes, nothing to say that he condemned or approved Ryker's decision. Placed in the same situation, though, Ryker believed they would have all made the same choice he had. No werewolf would give their mate up without a fight because all of them knew that life didn't mean shit without their mates by their side.

"We can't remove the ventilator from Amanda until she can breathe on her own," Doctor Brown continued, turning away to lead them to her door. "Which means she's incapable of taking your blood, which we all know is essential to the conversion. So we're going to do something that has never been done before, at least in the history of Wolf Town. Ryker, we're going to hook you up directly to her IV line. And after you've bitten her we are going to open your line, so your blood flows directly into hers."

They walked into the room. Ryker swallowed hard when he saw her, but he forced his mind to move past his grief. Doctor Sanders pulled a variety of supplies from the drawers and cabinets on the other side of the room as Doctor Brown did a last minute check of Amanda's vitals.

"Before I left, you had something to tell me," Ryker said, inhaling deeply. "What was it?"

Doctor Brown stepped away from the bed. "It's obsolete now, but I'd suspected that Amanda was your mate. It turns out I was right."

Ryker nodded. "You'll need to change first," Doctor Sanders told him, placing what he needed on a stainless steel cart with wheels. "We have to have the line in you before you bite her. It's essential that we use live blood from you, straight from the source. I don't think it would work if we took it from you in advance. After you've changed, we need you remain in wolf form until we remove the IV. It won't take us long, we don't want to overwhelm her system with your blood."

"Then what?" Ryker asked as he undressed.

"Then we wait," Doctor Sanders replied, his voice carefully flat. "Go ahead and change and I'll get you hooked up."

The room was quiet as Ryker followed the doctor's orders. Once he was in wolf form, a small area of his front shoulder was shaved with clippers. It was followed by a wet swab and a pinch. The IV was in.

"It's now or never," Doctor Brown told him, moving around the bed to stand next to Ivan. Ryker nodded his large head, his eyes settling on her calf. As gently as possible he leaned forward to pierce her skin with one fang, just enough to allow a thin trail of blood to well out of her leg.

Lapping at it gently, he allowed the words that would change her to come forth in his mind. *By the power of the moon and the bond that has united our life forces, I share my blood and wolf essence consensually with my mate.*

He released her leg. Doctor Sanders opened the line, Ryker's blood quickly filling the clear tubing. It disappeared into her arm. Amanda remained motionless, with no visible reaction to his words or blood.

The doctor removed the needle from his shoulder before disposing of it. "You can change now," he told Ryker, cleaning up the area around them.

With just a thought, Ryker was human again. "Why isn't she reacting?" he asked quietly, pulling on his jeans. She looked exactly as she had before, her chest rising and falling unnaturally.

The other three men stared back at him with sympathy on their faces. "You just have to be patient, Ryker," Ivan finally replied, in a kind voice. "We're moving in uncharted territory here. We just have to wait and see."

Ryker nodded before pulling a chair next to the bed and grasping her hand gently. "Whatever happens, I'm in this with you," he vowed to her in a low voice, his mouth close to her ear. "Even if I have to follow you into death itself."

Then he settled back into his seat with his eyes locked on her face, watching and waiting to see where she'd end up leading them.

Epilogue

One month later...

Amanda smiled at the customer as he turned away to return to his table, checking to see if anyone else needed a drink. For the moment, the patrons were happy. The bar was busy, but not extremely so. Amanda liked it best when it was like that, it allowed her to keep a more comfortable pace.

Jean waved at her from the end of the bar, motioning for her to come over and join her. "Come over here and take a load off for awhile. You can always get back up, if someone needs something. We don't need you wearing yourself out."

Amanda nodded, sliding into her chair next to her. She'd only been back to work for a few days. She was still Jean's bookkeeper, but she'd agreed to bartend, too, if Jean ever found herself in a pinch. It had happened sooner than she'd expected. Her help for that night had called in sick, so Amanda had volunteered to come in and take her place.

"I still can't believe you're back," Jean confided, squeezing her hand warmly before releasing it. "I have to admit I thought you were a goner that night you collapsed. I never dreamed your cancer would go into remission, especially once you fell into the coma. Thank God Ryker has the connections he does. Had he not got you into the doctors he knows, I doubt you'd even be alive today, much less back here at the Red Ruby."

It was the story Ryker and Amanda had agreed upon, and the only one that allowed her to return back to her old life. "Ryker, he's a good man," she confessed to Jean, smiling happily. "I don't know how I ever got lucky enough to land him, but somehow I did."

"Why not?" Jean asked her, lifting her cigarette from the ashtray to puff on it. "You're a good woman, and you deserve the best. Someone else up there must think so, too," she added, pointing to the ceiling. "Not very many people get the second chance you have, so use it wisely."

"Absolutely," Amanda agreed, turning her head to check on her customers. If only the other woman knew how much of a second chance she'd really gotten. After coming back from the coma, Ryker had confessed what he was before telling her what he'd done to save her. At first, Amanda had thought she was hallucinating, but once he'd changed in front of her eyes she'd realized the truth of his words.

It had taken her time to adjust to the fact that she, too, was now a werewolf. She hadn't changed into one yet, but Ryker thought she would soon. She'd been converted at the very brink of death, and according to him, it would take her wolf time to establish itself comfortably. Amanda was fine with that. She was still trying to adapt herself.

The most astonishing fact of all had been discovering Ryker loved her. The transition from lovers to a true relationship had happened easily. It just felt right. Amanda couldn't imagine a future without him in it. And she wouldn't have to. They were mates.

Ryker had taken her into Wolf Town several times, not only introducing her to the residents but acclimating her to her new way of life. She was impressed. They'd welcomed her with open arms. Ryker had no desire to move back into the settlement, though, and truth be told, neither did she. Amanda enjoyed having him all to herself. For once, her life was picture perfect.

"What about that sister of yours?" Jean spat out, her voice filled with her dislike of the other woman. "Have you heard anything from her?"

"No, and I'm sure I never will," Amanda said sadly. Her sister had made her feelings about her extremely clear when she'd signed the paperwork to end her life. "I suppose she thinks I'm dead so why disappoint her? As much as I hate how bad things are between us, I don't see us ever being close. We never have been, and it's a little too late for that now."

"It's not your fault. There are some people you can never win, no matter how hard you try."

The door opened. In the mirror, Amanda watched as Pat walked in. She grinned as his eyes settled on Jean's back. He immediately headed in their direction.

"Looks like your sweetie is coming," Amanda teased Jean as she got up from her chair. The older woman turned her head to peek before focusing on the television again. Her cheeks turned pink as a small smile played about her lips. Jean was playing hard to get, but it was working. It was clear the older man was crazy about her... and clearly she wasn't immune to his charms either.

Amanda walked away to take another drink order. Just as she took his money the door opened again. Expecting to see a customer, she was filled with pleasure at the sight of Ryker's large frame walking across the room. He wasn't alone. The door remained open as person after person filed in behind him. She immediately recognized most of them from Wolf Town.

Ryker was followed by Alexander and his very pregnant wife Carole Anne, and Marrok and Connor and their mates. Even Doctor Sanders was with them, staring around the bar with an appreciative expression on his face. Ryker stopped right in front of her, a huge grin on his face.

"What can I get you?" Amanda teased him, her heart thumping loudly at the sight of him. She doubted she'd ever get over how gorgeous he was... or the fact that he was hers.

"How about the rest of your life?" Ryker asked, coming down to one knee in front of the bar. He opened a black box before extending his arm to show it to her. Inside was a gorgeous diamond ring, the setting much larger than any she'd seen before. She gaped at it in surprise before staring at his face.

"Over the last several months, you've come to mean everything to me. And although we've faced more obstacles than many see in a lifetime, they've only made my feelings for you grow stronger. I can honestly say that fate has destined me for you, and you for me. Amanda, will you agree to marry me?"

Her eyes filled with tears at his heartfelt words and the sincerity shining is his deep blue eyes. "Yes," she replied happily, clasping her hands together in front of her in joy as she all but jumped up and down in delight.

Ryker came to his feet easily. He pulled the ring out of the box before taking her left hand in his and sliding it onto her finger. It was a perfect fit.

"Thank God," he said loudly, leaning forward until their faces were only inches apart. "After letting you take my body for a test drive these last few weeks, I was worried you were never going to buy it." Several of the werewolves behind him chuckled, while Connor hollered out, "If she were smart she wouldn't." They all laughed, even Amanda.

"You weren't laughing last night," Ryker whispered to Amanda with a grin, his hand sliding behind her head to cup it as he pulled her in for a kiss. When their lips met, everyone else faded away. What existed between them was magical, but it was also addictive. She doubted she'd ever get enough of him, even if she did live for several lifetimes.

They pulled away from each other smiling. The whole bar erupted in cheers, news of the proposal having quickly spread throughout the tables. "Congratulations, sweetie," Jean said from next to her, pulling her into a hug with a huge smile on her face.

Amanda laughed when she saw the supposedly-sick bartender standing next to her. "Let me guess, this was all a set up?" she asked, shaking her head in amusement.

"Of course," Jean replied, winking at her. "Ryker called me yesterday and asked me to help him. Naturally, I couldn't resist. You deserve all of this and more, honey. Now go out there and get it."

Impulsively, Amanda hugged her again before walking around the bar and into Ryker's opened arms. Several members of the pack stepped up to congratulate them, some of them even hugging Amanda. And for the first time in years she finally felt loved and accepted. It didn't matter if they were related by blood or not. The odd mix of humans and werewolves were her family.

"Enough of this," Connor said in a loud voice. "If I have to see anymore of this mushy shit, I'm going to puke. I need a beer. In fact, I'm buying a round for the whole bar!"

Amidst the cheers, Jean stared at Connor wide-eyed before meeting Amanda's eyes. "I really like this man," she told her, from across the bar. "Hurry," she hissed to the new bartender. "Get their orders before he changes his mind."

Amanda laughed, happier than she'd ever been in her life. It was amazing how quickly things could change, all in the span of a few short months.

"You never told me that Jean's new male friend

was Pat," Ryker said, close to her ear.

"You know him?" she asked, surprised.

"Oh, yeah," he replied, a grin in his voice. "He's pack."

Holy shit. Amanda's eyes widened as she stared at the older man before looking at Jean. The other woman was oblivious. Connor had made her night with his extremely large drink order, and she was making sure that *everyone* got something. Finally, Amanda chuckled. Life really was unpredictable, but she was certainly enjoying the ride.

"Have I told you today how much I love you?" she asked, turning to wind her arms around Ryker's neck.

Ryker pretended to think about it. "I don't think so," he replied, pulling her close. "Maybe you should refresh my memory."

"I love you," she replied simply. "And I'm grateful I got the chance to."

"Oh, God," Connor called out in mock horror. "I can't even turn my back on them for a moment without them groping each other. He looked down at the pregnant female next to him. "Natalie, they're even worse than we are." His mate blushed as she elbowed him. Hard.

Marrok crossed his arms before making a loud sound of disgust. "Worse than you are?" he repeated, in a loud voice. "Really, Connor? I don't see them rolling around in the hay like animals."

The guardians erupted in laughter as someone

put a beer in Connor's hand. "Man, he busted your balls," Orlando said, laughing so hard he had to hold his side.

Ryker rolled his eyes before looking down at Amanda. "Now you see why I left Wolf Town," he told her, his arm wrapped tightly around her waist.

"I'm glad you did."

"I'm glad I did, too," he replied sincerely, his warm eyes sliding over her face. "It was the best decision I ever made. I found a lot more than peace out in that house. I also found my future, my very reason for living."

"Me, too," she whispered back, her heart bursting with love.

Other Books By Rose Wynters:

Wolf Town Guardians: Born to walk this world as both wolf and human, these men take their role as protectors very seriously. Enjoying sensual pleasures as they please, this group of alpha werewolves are the finest when it comes to protecting their hidden settlement.

Guardians are the masters of self-control, taking pride in their authority and hard, muscled bodies. That all changes at the first scent of their mates. Their control snaps. The mating heat begins.

This is their stories.

Book One: My Wolf King
Book Two: My Wolf Protector
Book Three: My Wolf Cowboy
Book Four: My Wolf Fighter

The Endurers: Once upon a time, the world was just a black void. Then one day man came, but he wasn't alone. He was followed by an ancient evil, a scourge determined to steal his soul. Centuries passed. Humanity did all it could to protect itself against the evil ones, but they weren't equipped to fight this battle. Instead, all they could do was pray that Hell didn't set its eyes upon them.

It got to be too much. Something had to be done.

Born out of desperate need, warriors were chosen. Immortality was granted to those strong enough to fight the battle that would never end. No longer mortal, these men have stood in the path of dark and horrifying evil, bearing the load when there was nobody else that could.

It's all coming to an end. Time has run out for humanity...

> Book One: Rubenesque Rapture
> Book Two: Curvaceous Condemnation
> Book Three: Delicate Devastation
> Book Four: Voluptuous Vindication

Territory Of The Dead: *The world as she knew it is over...*

Working as a checkout girl in the small town of Pleasant, LA, Tabitha never dreamed her job as a cashier would turn bloody. But when zombies take over the town, Tabitha becomes a survivor. She quickly learns that being eighteen isn't all it's cracked up to be... especially when the entire world is out to kill—or eat—you.

> Phase One: Identify
> Phase Two: Evaluate
> Phase Three: Devastate
> Phase Four: Analyze

The Vampire's House of Pleasure Series:
Violet was fascinated with the legends and lore of New Orleans. She was so fascinated that she left

everything behind to run a B&B in the French Quarter. But she never imagined that vampires were really real... not until the night she found herself swept back in time to 1797.

Beaten and scared, Violet quickly realizes she's trapped—and in the most exotic bordello of all. But its clients aren't mortal, at least not anymore. Locked in an era that's not her own, there's no way to escape the society filled with debauchery, voodoo, and the powerful lure of vampire seductiveness... but Violet must find a way to return to her own time—before it's too late.

    Part One
    Part Two
    Part Three

Made in the USA
Middletown, DE
26 August 2016